"Don't cry, darling. Please don't cry. I'm a good guy. And I can see you're a good girl..."

They both went to sleep...eventually... though Luke took quite a while to come to terms with what had just happened. He hoped he was right. Hoped she *was* a good girl. If not, he'd just done the stupidest thing he'd ever done in his whole life. Slept with a perfect stranger. Then, to top it all off, he'd fallen in love with her....

Dear Reader,

Love can be full of surprises!

We know you'll enjoy the last book in Miranda Lee's bewitching trilogy, AFFAIRS TO REMEMBER. All three stories are about love affairs with a difference, and they are brought especially to you by this popular Australian author—all the tales have twists that you won't forget!

Sincerely,

The Editor

Books by Miranda Lee

Don't miss any of our special offers. Write to us at the following address for information on our newest releases.

Harlequin Reader Service
U.S.: 3010 Walden Ave., P.O. Box 1325, Buffalo, NY 14269
Canadian: P.O. Box 609, Fort Erie, Ont. L2A 5X3

MIRANDA LEE

A Woman to Remember

Harlequin Books

TORONTO • NEW YORK • LONDON
AMSTERDAM • PARIS • SYDNEY • HAMBURG
STOCKHOLM • ATHENS • TOKYO • MILAN
MADRID • WARSAW • BUDAPEST • AUCKLAND

ISBN 0-373-11861-9

A WOMAN TO REMEMBER

First North American Publication 1997.

Printed in U.S.A.

PROLOGUE

SHE took the clothes from the case and laid them out on the hotel bed: a leopardskin-print halter-necked mini-dress, sexy gold sandals with outrageously high heels plus the obligatory ankle strap, and a cream stretch satin G-string which would give the illusion of nakedness underneath the oh, so tight dress.

Not another thing. No bra. No stockings. No petticoat.

A shudder rippled through her at the thought of what she would look like dressed in that garb, with her long tawny blonde hair wildly fluffed out around her face and shoulders, her full mouth made to look even fuller with carefully applied lip-liner and filled in with the sort of lipstick it would take paint-stripper to remove.

Hardly subtle.

Still, that was what she wanted to look like. There was no time for her usual ladylike image. No time for demure or coy. She had only this one night. A few bare hours.

Dismay swept in at the thought of what she was going to do, of how she would have to act to get what she wanted so quickly and so thoroughly. Dear God, what had happened to her this past year? What had she become?

For a split-second she almost backed away from the idea, but desperation and a fierce frustration brought renewed resolve. She had to go home in the morning—home to her dying husband, home to nothing but more weeks of disappointment and despair and loneliness such as she'd never known before.

She could not let this chance go by. She had to grab it. She simply had to!

Snatching up the folded newspaper lying on the pillow, she rechecked the address of the photographic exhibition—the only opening she could find on that particular Wednesday night. It was not a street or a gallery she recognised, but there again it had been some years since she'd lived and worked in Sydney.

She jotted down the address, hoping against hope that this type of function would be the same as they'd always been—full of highly sociable swinging singles. Admittedly, a percentage of the seemingly available men—and often the best-looking—would be gay, but there would always be a sprinkling of straight males with more machismo than morals.

And where are *your* morals, Rachel? came the taunting inner question.

'I left them at home,' she snapped aloud as she threw the newspaper into the wastepaper basket. 'Along with everything else I once held dear. Life is a different ball-game these days. A different ball-game,' she bit out, her heart hardening as she strode quickly into the bathroom, dragging off her wedding ring as she went.

There was no time for guilt tonight. Or conscience. Or, God forbid, shame. Shame was for normal wives in normal situations. It had no place in her life at that moment. No place at all!

CHAPTER ONE

'YOU'LL have to go to the dentist.'

Luke popped the two painkillers into his mouth and swigged them back with a large glass of water.

'I'll go when I get back to Los Angeles,' he said, turning from the kitchen sink to smile at his still frowning mother. 'It's not that bad.'

Grace wasn't about to be distracted from her maternal mission, although she recognised that her son's smile would have distracted most of the female gender. Distract, disarm and downright disorientate.

At thirty-two, Luke had become a lethal weapon where his looks were concerned. Age and life had finally put some interesting lines on his once too smoothly handsome face, especially around his eyes and mouth, giving him more sex appeal than ever.

His two elder brothers were good-looking men, but Luke was matinée idol material, having inherited the best of his parents' genes—his father's tall, well-proportioned body, clear olive skin and flashing dark eyes, and his mother's symmetrical features, high cheekbones and sensually carved mouth. All in all, a potent mix.

As a teenage boy Grace's youngest son had been a big hit with girls. No doubt nowadays he was an equally big hit with women. Pity he couldn't find one to settle down with, Grace thought wryly.

Not that he mixed with the type of woman she would have chosen as a daughter-in-law. Luke's life as private and personal photographer to the stars in Hollywood meant that his immediate circle of acquaintance was the entertainment and movie-world crowd. Hardly the sort of people renowned for long-term commitment and traditional values.

Motherly concern had Grace wishing that one of these days Luke would come home to Australia to live permanently, not just pop home to Sydney for the odd week every year or so. He was an Aussie at heart, and she felt sure he'd be happier at home.

He never looked very happy these days. There were always dark smudges under his eyes, and his mouth had taken on a cynical twist which made her feel quite sad. The young man who'd flown off to see the world and make his fortune ten years ago had not been a cynic.

The man who'd flown in yesterday definitely was, and had been for quite some time. He also hadn't been too happy for quite some time.

Not that it was easy to be bright and bushy-tailed with jet-lag and a nagging tooth. Knowing how difficult men could be when something physical was wrong with them, Grace had no intention of letting Luke procrastinate over getting his tooth fixed.

'You don't fly back to LA till Sunday week,' she pointed out firmly. 'That's two whole weeks away. You can't put up with a toothache for that long. Now, don't be such a baby, Luke. Lord, I know you hated the dentist when you were a boy, but you're a grown man now.

'Fancy!' She tut-tutted, well aware that nothing prodded a man into action more quickly than a jab at his male ego. 'Thirty-two and still scared of the dentist.'

'I'm *not* scared of the dentist,' he shot back testily, all smiles abandoned. 'I simply don't like being in that damned chair. I detest how it makes you feel, sitting there. Totally out of control and at someone else's mercy!'

Grace glanced at the stubborn set of her youngest son's jaw and thought, Yes, you'd hate that, wouldn't you? You've always wanted to run your own race—always resented being pushed into corners. No one could ever make you do something you didn't want to do, or dissuade you from doing something you *did* want to do.

Still, Grace had to admit that she admired Luke's tunnel vision and tenacity. He'd dared to do what others had only dreamt about. He'd followed his dreams and made them come true. At least professionally speaking. Privately, his life hadn't been so successful. She wondered what had happened to that young actress he'd been living with a couple of years back. Luke's letters had indicated that marriage was imminent, but then suddenly nothing.

Grace would never forget how grim he had looked when he'd flown home a couple of months later. And how bitter he'd become about women. He hadn't confided in her, of course. Boys gave up confiding in their mothers at around the same time they discovered the opposite sex. With Luke that had been a good twenty years ago.

But his being his own man didn't stop her being his mother, and wanting to do mother-type things for him.

'Going to the dentist is not as bad as it used to be,' she argued reasonably. 'The new drills are practically painfree, and they have that gas which helps a lot if you're the tense type.'

'They still stuff sixty million wads of cotton wool in your mouth so that you can't speak properly,' Luke returned irritably. 'Then there's that damned hook thing, which makes the most appalling sucking noises—not to mention the way it drags the corner of your mouth down so that you look like some mutant from Mars.'

Grace chuckled. 'So that's the root of the problem. You simply don't want to look less than your gorgeous best for Dr Evans's pretty little dental nurse.'

Luke's left eyebrow lifted with a mildly sardonic interest. 'Does Dr Evans have a pretty little dental nurse?'

'He did the last time I went. Goodness, if I'd known I'd have mentioned her earlier. So you've still got a weakness for pretty women, have you?'

His glance was sharp, confirming Grace's opinion that some pretty woman had hurt her son once—hurt him badly. She wondered if it had been the actress.

'I've moved on from pretty to gorgeous these days,' he said drily.

'And is there one particular gorgeous girl in your life I should know about?' Grace asked.

'Nope.'

It was a bit like pulling teeth, Grace thought, trying to get information out of Luke. 'What happened to that Tracy girl you used to write me about?' she persisted. 'It sounded like you were going to marry her at one stage.'

'I was. But in the end she decided to embrace her acting career rather than yours truly,' came his coldly caustic remark.

'Why did she have to make a choice? I thought American girls tried to have it all. Marriage and children, *and* a career.'

Luke's laugh was hard. 'Don't go believing those sitcoms you see on television, Mum. That's fantasyland. Tracy didn't mind the marriage bit. She quite fancied being Mrs Luke St Clair. But she drew the line at babies, and at least she was honest enough to say so up front. I didn't see the point in marriage without children, so we called it quits.'

'And rightly so. Marriage without children for you would be a disaster. You'd make a great father.'

He seemed taken aback, throwing her a surprised look. 'What makes you say that?'

'Oh, Luke, don't be silly. I'm your mother. I know these things.'

'Aah. Feminine instinct, is it?'

'Maternal instinct. And paternal example. Your father was a great father. His sons take after him in that regard.'

'Well, that's too bad, because I'm afraid I don't see myself marrying now, let alone having kiddies.'

'You really loved Tracy that much?'

'Good God, no! I'm well and truly over that ambitious little bitch.'

'Then what is it, Luke?' she asked, genuinely confused. 'You're only thirty-two. You've still plenty of time to get married and have a family.'

An awkward silence descended on the kitchen while Luke rubbed his jaw and frowned darkly.

'Who is she?' Grace said abruptly. 'Another actress?'

Exasperation sent dangerous lights glittering in his deeply set black eyes. 'This is exactly why I don't tell you anything, Mum,' he bit out. 'Before I know it, I'm getting the third degree. Let's drop the subject of women all round, shall we? I've come home for a nice, relaxing holiday—not to face a modern version of the Spanish Inquisition!'

'I only have your best interests at heart,' Grace defended herself. 'I only want you to be happy— like Mark and Andy.'

Luke glared at her for a moment longer, before a rueful smile smoothed the frustration from his face. Walking over, he took his mother into his arms and gave her a big hug.

'I am not unhappy, Mum,' he said. 'Hell, what have I got to be unhappy about? Other than this damned tooth, of course,' he added, grimacing.

Grace could see that she wasn't going to get any more out of him about his love life. But she wasn't going to let him off the hook so easily where the dentist was concerned.

'In that case I'm not going to take any more nonsense from you,' she said staunchly. 'I'm going to ring up and make you an appointment at the dentist. If I say it's an emergency they're sure to fit you in some time this morning. I'll drive you down to the surgery myself. I've got some shopping to do and I can do it while you're in there.'

'Oh, all right,' Luke grumbled. 'I can see you're determined, and if there's one thing I know about my mother it's that she can't be swayed once she sets her mind on something. You're as stubborn as a mule!'

Takes one to know one, Grace thought wryly as she left the room and made her way to the telephone.

Ten o'clock found Luke in the passenger side of his mother's battered old blue sedan, feeling rather ambivalent about where they were going. He'd lied to his mother when he'd said that he wasn't afraid of the dentist. He was.

But thirty-two-year-old men couldn't admit to such failings. They couldn't admit to anything which other people might jump on and make fun of, which men might use against them or—worse— which women might look down upon.

Being a real man was a bloody lonely business sometimes, Luke conceded drily to himself. Real men didn't moan or groan. Or enter therapy. They certainly didn't cry on their mother's shoulders.

Hell, no! A real man looked life straight in the eye and didn't blink an eyelid in the face of adversity. No matter what, he forged on—strong and silent and self-sufficient!

Damn, but he hated being a real man sometimes—especially when going to the rotten dentist!

'I have no idea why you won't let me buy you a new car,' he grumped as his mother backed out of the garage. 'Or a new house,' he added, scowling up into the sky as a jumbo jet roared overhead, the noise deafening.

'I like living in Monterey,' his mother returned, exasperation in her voice. 'I've lived here all my married life. Your father and I were very happy living in this house. I raised you and your two brothers in this house. Most of my friends live round here. Not only that, your father's buried not two miles down the road, and I—'

'All right, all right. I get the point,' Luke broke in frustratedly. 'I just wanted to do something for you, Mum, that's all.' He adored his mother. And admired her enormously.

She hadn't gone to pieces when a heart attack had left her a widow five years ago after nearly forty years of happy marriage—hadn't asked any of her sons to let her live with them. She'd picked herself up and gone on with her life, filling the lonely hours with lots of volunteer work and generally being a fantastic person.

But she could be a bit of a pain once she got her teeth into something.

'You *can* do something for me, Luke,' she piped up suddenly, and Luke shot her a wary glance.

'What?'

'Come back to Australia to live. I'm sure once you get home you'll find a nice girl who'll be more than happy to marry you and have all the children you want.'

Luke felt a deep, dark emotion well up inside him, but he dampened it down, hiding his feelings as best he could. Impossible to tell her that he *had* found a girl, here in Sydney, the last time he'd been home.

Unfortunately she hadn't been at all nice. Neither had she been the type to settle down and have children.

But, for all that, Luke had not been able to forget her afterwards. Not for a minute. She obsessed him every waking moment, haunted his dreams and was slowly destroying his peace of mind.

His mother talked of his seeming unhappy. How could he be happy when he didn't know who he was any more, or where he was going with his life? He'd been lost since he'd woken that morning eighteen months ago to find her gone. He'd searched and searched, but could find no trace. It was almost as though she'd never existed.

But she *had* existed. He only had to close his eyes and the memories would sweep in. Her face. Her passion. The all-consuming heat of her beautiful body.

God, if only she would let him go! If only he could stop remembering!

'Luke?' his mother prompted. 'Don't go giving me the silent treatment. I can't stand it when one of my boys goes all quiet and brooding on me.'

Luke pulled himself together, finding a cool mask from somewhere to turn towards his far too intuitive mother.

'I would have thought Andy and Mark had more than adequately fulfilled your grandmothering needs, Mum,' he pointed out drily. 'They have five very nice children between them—three boys and two girls—plus two perfect daughters-in-law for wives. You really don't need me to add to the St Clair brood, or the St Clair wives. Two out of three ain't bad, you know. Don't become one of those meddling matchmaking mums, or I might be forced to stay in LA in future.'

Her hurt look made him feel instantly guilty, and he sighed his regret. 'Just kidding, Mum. You know you're my best girl. I could never stay away from you for too long.'

'Flatterer,' she said, but he could see that she was pleased.

His mother mollified, Luke sat back silently and tried to distract his wretched mind by focusing on the familiar but still beautiful surroundings. He stared out at the blue waters of Botany Bay on their right, then up at the clear blue sky. Nowhere in the world had he ever found skies such as in Australia. Their clearness and brightness was unique, but it made for harsh light—not the easiest background for good photography.

It took special skills and equipment to photograph Australian scenery really well—unless one captured the shots at dawn or dusk—skills which he had never honed, but which could present an interesting challenge, Luke decided unexpectedly.

His passion had always been photographing people, right from his boyhood days. He'd perfected portraiture, especially in black and white, and had made a small fortune out of it.

There'd been a time when he'd got a kick out of surprising people with his flattering photographs of them. Models and actresses with a portfolio by Luke St Clair had a definite edge in the cut-throat world of auditions in the US. He was sought-after and paid handsomely for his work. He could command huge fees.

But, quite frankly, it had all become somewhat of a bore.

Besides, he no longer needed to do things for money. An inspired investment in a small independent movie which had taken the world by storm a couple of years back had ensured he never had to work again if he didn't want to. So perhaps it was time to spread his photographic wings, so to speak. To find a new direction to satisfy his creative eye.

Maybe his mother was right, he began to muse. Maybe it was time to come home—if not to marry then to find a new life-path. He could not go on as he had this past year. It was slowly destroying him.

'I'll let you out here,' his mother suggested, pulling over to the kerb. 'The dentist is just in that small arcade over there. There's a narrow staircase which leads up to a corridor, and his surgery is the second door on the left upstairs. I'll meet you in that coffee-shop on the corner. Whichever one of us gets there first can wait for the other.'

Butterflies gathered in the pit of his stomach as he mounted the stairs and pushed open the glass door. A very attractive brunette looked up from behind the reception desk, saw the cut of the man standing there and smiled a smile as old as time itself.

'Yes, can I help you?' she asked hopefully.

Luke did his best to ignore the silent invitation in her pretty blue eyes, despite his own gaze automatically shifting to her left hand. He was almost relieved to see a diamond engagement ring twinkling there, for in all truth he'd become horribly addicted to picking up pretty women during the last year or so, taking them out, then home to bed, then never contacting them again.

He wasn't proud of his behaviour, but he understood it. He was punishing them for *her*.

He excused himself by saying that he only picked up the really eager ones—the ones who made it perfectly obvious what they wanted from him. Like *she* had. He always hoped to gain some darkly twisted satisfaction from being the one who did the seducing and the dumping. Instead he always felt like a rat in the morning, hating himself more and more with each episode.

The women involved didn't know it, but they were better off without him. He'd become a right bastard—sexually speaking—since that night, his only concession to his conscience being that he steered clear of married and engaged women. He took some small comfort from that, soothing his escalating qualms with the thought that he hadn't descended to being a complete scoundrel yet.

'My name's St Clair,' he announced, deliberately leaving off the Luke. 'I have an appointment for ten-thirty.'

'Oh, yes, Mr St Clair. I'm afraid Dr Evans is running a little late. Maybe fifteen minutes or so. Would you like some tea or coffee while you wait?'

Tea or coffee on his churning stomach? A whisky, perhaps, but he didn't think she'd offer him that. 'No thanks,' came his brusque reply. 'I'll just wait.'

'There are plenty of magazines,' she told him as he walked over to settle himself into one of the black leather two-seaters which lined the starkly white walls.

Luke did his best to relax, resting his right ankle on his left knee and spreading his arms along the back of the seat. But he soon found his fingers tapping impatiently on the leather. In the end he picked up one of the dog-eared women's weeklies lying on the table next to him, smiling wryly when he saw that it was dated four years previously.

He began idly flicking through it, just to pass the time, and might have missed her picture altogether if his attention hadn't been attracted by the headline

above it: MODEL GIVES UP BLOSSOMING CAREER
TO MARRY NOTED SCIENTIST.

It had been years since Luke had made his living
doing fashion magazine layouts, but during that
time many of his friends had been models—and
some had been more than friends—so curiosity had
him open the double page in his lap and look to
see if this particular model was anyone he knew.

His eyes skimmed the kissing couple to see if he
recognised them, but it was impossible with their
faces obscured—though he noted that the bride-
groom had greying hair. So he scanned the words
beneath, looking for names.

No bells rang in his brain when he read that a
twenty-two-year-old model named Rachel Manning
had married noted geneticist Patrick Cleary at St
Mary's Cathedral, Sydney, that Saturday afternoon
four years previously. It was only when his gaze
dropped further, to another smaller photograph of
the bride alone, that he recognised her.

Had he gone as white as a sheet?

Luke fancied that he had.

His knuckles certainly went white as his fingers
tightened around the pages, his eyes wide upon the
photograph of the smiling bride—the gloriously
golden-haired and exquisitely beautiful bride.

How innocent she looked in her white bridal
gown, he thought savagely. The picture of perfect
purity. The very essence of untouched womanhood.

A rage began to grow inside him as his shock
gave way to anger. She'd been *married*! The bitch
had been *married*!

My God, it explained so much. So damned much!

There had been so many elements of that night which had stayed to haunt him. So many unanswered questions.

Now he had the answers.

Or did he?

Just because she'd been married four years ago it didn't mean that she'd still been married eighteen months ago. There was such a thing as divorce, wasn't there? Maybe she wasn't an adulterous little tramp. Maybe there were other reasons why she'd acted the way she had that night—why she'd chosen to disappear while he was asleep, without leaving a trace of her true identity.

And maybe pigs might fly, came the blackly cynical thought.

'Dr Evans is ready for you now, Mr St Clair.'

Luke schooled his face into what he hoped was a normal expression, snapped the magazine shut and placed it back on the pile in the corner.

Forget her, common sense whispered. She's bad news.

He stood up and walked over to where the dental nurse was waiting for him in the now open doorway. Her petite prettiness didn't even register. He no longer felt nervous either. *She* dominated his mind again, turning his thoughts from the present.

Luke distractedly settled in the dental chair and closed his eyes, his mind whirling with memories. But how could he forget her now? Now that she had a name.

Rachel.

He hadn't known her name when she'd picked him up at the exhibition that night eighteen months ago. Hadn't known it the next morning, when he'd woken to find her gone.

Rachel...

It didn't suit her, he decided viciously.

Oh, it suited the bride in the photograph, but not the sultry feline creature who had undulated into his sight that night. Rachel sounded like a lady— but it had been no lady who'd boldly approached him within seconds of spotting him leaning against a pillar, who'd stolen his drink from his hands and taken a deep swallow, who'd smiled seductively at him over the rim before uttering the most astonishingly forthright proposal he'd ever heard from a woman.

And he'd heard a good few in his time.

The dentist was talking to him as he worked, but Luke didn't hear a word. He was back at that exhibition, hearing her say those astonishing words again, reliving every moment of that unforgettable but ultimately soul-destroying night.

CHAPTER TWO

'I HAVE a hotel room nearby,' she said in a huskily sexy voice, her incredible green eyes locked to his all the while. 'If you're as bored as you look, perhaps you'd like to join me there.'

Luke straightened, glad that his drink now rested between those long, elegant fingers with the equally long bronze-tipped nails. Otherwise he would surely have spilt his drink down his front. Though perhaps that might not have been such a bad idea. Things were happening down there which could do with a spot of cooling down.

He stared deep into those exotic green pools, because it was safer than looking at the rest of her. Not that he hadn't already had a damned good look as she'd slowly sashayed towards him across the gallery floor.

She had a stunning face—exotic perfection framed by a wild tawny blonde mane—but an even more than stunning body. Tall and slender, with high, firm breasts, a riveting cleavage and long, long legs which ran right up to her tiny waist. Or so it seemed.

Dressed a touch obviously for his usual taste in women, her leopardskin-print mini left nothing to the imagination. Hell, if she was wearing anything underneath he couldn't spot it. The silky material

24

clung like a second skin, the halter-necked style leaving her shoulders and arms bare, the short, short skirt showing an expanse of firm tanned thigh which would do a stripper proud.

This last thought made him wonder what she *did* do for a living. Though perhaps it was better if he didn't know.

Normally he was attracted to cool, classy types, sophisticated career women who exuded an understated and challenging sexuality which left it up to him to do the chasing. They sent out silent and very subtle messages for him to follow. They didn't openly invite, like this bold creature.

'Are you in the habit of propositioning perfect strangers?' he drawled, trying not to sound as shocked as he was feeling. Or as aroused.

He told himself that it was because he hadn't been with a woman since he'd broken up with Tracy a couple of months before. But underneath he knew this wasn't so. He'd wanted this she-cat the moment he'd set eyes on her.

A slight frown drew her perfectly arched eyebrows close together. 'You're American,' she said.

He could have enlightened her, but something... some indefinable tension which this mistaken conclusion was evoking in her, made him keep his Australian heritage to himself. He'd been told that he'd picked up an American accent, but he hadn't believed it till that moment.

'You don't like Americans?' he asked, taking the drink back from her suddenly still hands and draining it dry. He had a feeling he might need to be a little drunk to get through this evening.

'That depends,' she said, a touch warily. 'Are you holidaying here? Or staying indefinitely?'

'Holidaying,' he said, quite truthfully. But I might stay indefinitely, came the dark thought. If it means I can spend every night with you.

Already he could feel the blood rushing hotly to his loins. Already...

His flesh might have become a painful and obvious embarrassment if he hadn't been wearing a longer-line sports jacket loosely over casually fitted dark trousers which also had plenty of room. Luke could put up with the discomfort, if it was his alone to contemplate and suffer in private.

He had no intention of letting this feline huntress see that he was ready prey for her animal-like sexuality. As much as he was turned on by her amazingly forward approach and absolutely knock-out body, his male ego insisted that he play hard to get for a decent amount of time.

At least a minute, came the drily self-mocking thought.

'Does that disqualify me?' he said lazily.

'On the contrary,' she murmured, her husky voice rippling down his spine like a mink-gloved hand. 'I love tourists. Especially tall, dark, handsome ones with sexy black eyes. You are alone, aren't you? No little wife or girlfriend back at the hotel, or in the States?'

'I'm so alone,' he told her, trying to sound cool but feeling anything but, 'that it's positively indecent.'

'Nothing about you is indecent, handsome,' she murmured. 'You're positively gorgeous and positively perfect. Come with me . . .'

She pried the empty glass out of his suddenly frozen hand and bent to place it on the floor, giving him an uninterrupted view of her quite perfect breasts. Rising again, she smiled a siren's smile, slid her right hand into his still frozen left and began leading him away, across the upper gallery floor then down the wide white staircase.

The shredded remnants of Luke's common sense finally burst through his paralysed brain and he ground to a halt, momentarily resisting the hypnotic pull of the softly feminine fingers entwined through his.

'You're not a hooker, are you?' came his harsh-sounding question as they faced each other on the stairs.

He could not have mistaken the momentary shock which flared within those gorgeous green eyes, or his own inner shudder of relief. For what would he have done if she'd said that she was?

Still have gone with her, came the appalling admission.

'My mistake,' he muttered. 'Lead on, lover.' Obviously she was just a good-time girl, out on the tiles for the night. She wanted a one-night stand— without complications, without strings.

As much as that was not usually his style, Luke could see that it was going to be for tonight. It was no use pretending that he wasn't bowled over. *More* than bowled over. She seemed to have bewitched him with the primitive and alluring sexuality which emanated from every pore of her body. It wafted from her in waves, weaving a spell around his senses, teasing his flesh and his imagination, making him wonder what it would be like to spend the night with her.

She kept glancing over her shoulder at him as she drew him down the rest of the stairs and through the crowded foyer, her eyes sometimes smiling invitingly, sometimes seemingly checking that he was still there—as though she too could not believe he'd come with her so readily.

It was those glimpses of unexpected vulnerability which began intriguing Luke. The suspicion that this was not her usual style either began to form in his mind. She looked at him that way one time too many after they'd finally made it outside into the street, and he suddenly whipped her over into a darkened doorway, pulling her against him in a jolting embrace.

Her shocked gasp and almost frightened eyes confirmed his opinion that she was not used to playing such dangerous games. Either that, or she had never run into real trouble before.

'You little fool,' he snarled, infuriated by this last thought. 'Don't you know the risks you run in going off with a stranger?'

Her chin whipped up, green eyes glinting an answering fury at him. 'I take it you've changed your mind—is that it?' she snapped. 'If so, then say so, damn you.' She began to struggle to free herself from his arms. 'I have no time for cowards tonight.'

'Cowards! Why, you little...' Red spots of fury went off in his brain like flashlights, and before he knew it he'd grasped a large clump of her hair and yanked it back so that her chin tipped up all the more.

Before she could do more than cry out through startled lips, his mouth clamped down over those lips and he was kissing her as he'd never kissed a woman before. With anger, not passion, with a desire to punish and hurt, not seduce.

But seduction was the final result.

His, not hers. For as his tongue drove repeatedly into the depths of her mouth she moaned a moan which moved him as no woman's moan had ever done before, making him want to protect her, not punish her. Hold, not hurt.

He found it impossible to keep kissing her with such ferocity. His tongue gentled to a series of sinuous slides against hers, his free hand finding the small of her back and pressing inwards. He thrilled to the feel of her sinking weakly against him, then to the sound of another longer, more sensual moan—this one signalling total surrender to his male domination over her body. It brought a dizzying sense of sexual power, and he simply could not wait to have her naked and trembling beneath him.

'This hotel room,' he muttered thickly against her mouth. 'Is it far?'

She shook her head in the negative, the movement brushing her lush lips to and fro across his.

He shuddered as a rush of blood almost had him doing what he hadn't done since he was fifteen. Gulping, he drew back from the raw heat of her body to stare down into wildly dilated green eyes. She looked...stunned, he realised. Stunned, and totally at his mercy. It was an exhilarating and intoxicating thought—a male fantasy come true. Impossible to resist.

'Then take me there,' he muttered. 'And take me there quickly...'

The drill contacting his tooth brought Luke back to the present—physically at least—but his mind continued to churn over his still vivid memories.

Had she deceived him with that air of vulnerability, with her seemingly mindless surrender? Had she been so diabolically clever, so skilled in seducing strangers that she had made it seem as if *he* had been master of what had happened that evening? Whereas in reality *she* had been the one pulling the strings and making all the moves?

He desperately wanted to believe that she hadn't been married at the time—although it seemed likely that she had. Given that assumption, he clung to the idea that it had been her first foray into adultery.

Even so, he could not deny that she had come to that exhibition right and ready for a night of casual sex, dressed for the occasion and armed to the eye-teeth with the equipment necessary to reduce fools like him to instant mush.

Looking back, he could see that she'd also gone to great pains to protect her true identity—to cut down the risk of ever being caught out in her outrageous behaviour. She'd wanted a mad fling of some kind, but she hadn't wanted any evidence of that mad fling left behind. The only part of the puzzle which remained was why she'd taken that appalling risk during the middle of the night.

It couldn't have been deliberate, he decided, unless it had been part of some crazy fantasy she'd wanted to fulfil. He preferred to think that she'd simply been carried away—as *he* had been carried away.

It was one of the reasons why she haunted him. Because he'd never been carried away like that before. Or since...

'I don't even known your name,' he said when he finally closed the hotel room door, neither of them having said a word as she had led him swiftly down two blocks and into the foyer of a small but surprisingly elegant hotel. Not at all the sort of place for a cheap rendezvous.

The lift-ride up to the third floor had been tense, the presence of another man in the lift stifling any conversation or physical contact. Luke had hardly been aware of his surroundings as he'd eagerly followed her down the corridor. He had absorbed little but a brief impression of red-patterned carpet and black and white prints of ships on the walls.

'My name?' she repeated, almost as though she were in a fog.

He liked her disorientation, liked the way she gasped when he pulled her abruptly into his arms. 'Never mind,' he growled. 'No names for tonight. We'll exchange names in the morning.'

He kissed her again before the fog could lift.

God, but he liked the woman his kisses turned her into, liked the sounds she made under them, liked the feel of her lips melting along with her body. He'd never known a woman become so pliant in his arms before. Her sweet surrender to his mouth and hands filled him with the heady power to do as he pleased with her.

He pleased to take off all her clothes. What little there was of them.

He pleased to carry her over to the king-sized bed and stretch her, seemingly dazed, out on top of it.

He certainly pleased to sit beside her gloriously naked body and touch her all over... at will... and very, very thoroughly.

She didn't stop him, merely gazed up at him all the while with glazed green eyes, her lush lips gasping apart occasionally. Her pleasure was obvious, as was a bewildering amount of surprise. Hadn't she expected to enjoy his touch so much? Or was it that she wasn't used to a man giving her pleasure first this way?

She was getting close, he knew; her thighs were beginning to tremble. When her back began to arch from the bed he stopped abruptly, and she moaned her frustration.

It was only when Luke stood up that he realised his breathing was as hard and fast as hers. God, he hadn't been this excited in years, he realised. Or this enthralled with a woman. Stripped of those sluttish clothes, she had taken on a totally different persona. There was nothing cheap about her any more. She was all classical curves and sweetly fragrant beauty. She was even a genuine blonde!

He couldn't wait to bury himself in those softly golden curls, to have those lovely long legs wrapped tightly around him, to see those lush lips form a gasping O at the moment of her orgasm.

Funny, he had no conscious thought of his own satisfaction—which was a first for him. In the past, his priority when making love to a woman had always been what *he* would get out of it.

But not this time. This time he wanted to give even more than to receive.

Luke hardly recognised the man he'd become since entering this room. He felt all-powerful, yet that power was tempered with a strange tenderness. If he hadn't known better, he might have thought he'd finally really fallen in love. Even if not, it was certainly an experience outside his normal realm of experiences.

He could not even remember the first time he'd made love to Tracy, though he'd fancied himself in love with her back then. Yet already he knew he would never forget this night, not as long as he lived.

'You haven't done this before, have you?' he remarked as he began undressing himself, slipping out of his jacket and draping it over one of the bedposts.

She licked her lips, her eyes wide upon his. 'Why do you say that?' Her voice was husky, as though desire had dried her mouth and throat. But not the rest of her. The rest of her was far from dry, he recalled, with a lurching in his stomach.

'You seem too nervous.'

'I'm no virgin,' she protested, though shakily.

'I never said you were.' But her gaze was definitely close to virginal as it clung to his half-naked body.

Luke found her mixture of fascination and fear a real turn-on. He knew he had a good body, knew it was well equipped to satisfy most women's fantasies. So there was no hesitation when he finally stripped off his underwear. He actually saw the swallowing action in her throat, and revelled in her reaction.

'Where have you put the condoms?' he said as he joined her on the bed, running a gently caressing hand down her body as he did so.

She quivered uncontrollably and closed her eyes.

'Hey,' he prompted, quietly but firmly. 'The condoms?'

Long lashes fluttered open; the green eyes were pained. 'Oh, God,' she groaned, shaking her head from side to side. 'I didn't think. I just didn't think.'

Her distress touched him, despite his flash of annoyance at her naïvety. He would have to make sure that she never did insane things like this again. There again, she wasn't going to have any lovers other than him after tonight. He was going to make sure of that. Come morning, there would be no more of this 'stranger' nonsense.

'It's all right,' he reassured her, trying not to sound irritated. 'I always keep one in my wallet.'

And that was what was annoying him. One. Only *one*! They would need more than one before this night was out. He tossed up between dressing now and finding a twenty-four-hour chemist or doing it later.

Later, his intense desire told him. *Much* later.

He could not wait another minute. Or even another moment.

'No!' she cried out when he swung his legs over onto the floor.

His glance over his shoulder carried impatience and puzzlement. 'No, what?'

'No, I can't,' she rasped. 'I can't . . .'

Luke had no intention of letting her change her mind at this point. It was beyond bearing just thinking about it.

'It's all right,' he murmured, turning back to cup her face with firm hands and stare deep into her anguished green eyes. 'I understand. You've only just realised what a very silly girl you've been tonight. But I'm a good guy. Really. I won't hurt you, loveliness. I'm going to make beautiful love to you,' he promised, pressing her back against the pillow and kissing her.

He kept on kissing her till she began clinging to him and squirming with renewed desire. But he didn't dare leave her even then, reinforcing his temporary triumph by sliding down her body and kissing her all over till she was beyond stopping him, even when he had to abandon her for a short while.

She reached for him when he returned to the bed, pulling him down on top of her and not letting him indulge in any further foreplay. By this time Luke was ready to explode anyway, so when she opened to him, winding her legs high around his back, there really wasn't any option.

He drove deep into her hot, honeyed flesh, shuddering with pleasure at her exquisite tightness. He'd barely moved within her when her first fierce contraction seized his flesh, and it was all too much. He could not hold back another second, tremors racking his body as he climaxed uncontrollably, his spasms totally in tune with hers, going on and on for simply ages.

At last it was over, and he sank down upon her, feeling sated with pleasure. Yet even in the aftermath there was more pleasure, a sweet intimacy rising between them as her arms stole around him then squeezed, holding him tightly to her flattened breasts. His lips nuzzled her left ear and she sighed her satisfaction with him. He felt deliciously loved and loving, every limb and muscle flooded with a warm and wondrous peace.

He never wanted to leave her, but he had to in the end, though he returned from the *en suite* bathroom as quickly as possible. He began to see what the Bible meant about man and woman cleaving together to make one flesh. He felt only half a man away from her, already addicted to the feelings she evoked in him.

She was lying on her side watching him as he came back into the room, her position showing the delicious female curve of waist, hip and leg. Her breasts looked swollen, he noted, her nipples still hard, and her eyes were heavy-lidded and incredibly sensuous as they travelled slowly down his body.

His heart kicked over when her gaze drifted down past his navel, having an immediate effect on his till then flaccid flesh. The thought hit him immediately then he should dress and go in search of that chemist before another moment passed, but then she smiled that siren's smile at him and stretched out a beckoning hand. She drew him down onto the bed beside her and began to caress him with that hand, bringing him to full erection within an amazingly short time.

Transfixed by this sudden reversal of roles, Luke simply lay there, stunned and speechless as she continued to kiss and caress every inch of his body. There was nothing even remotely virginal about her now; everything she did was designed to tantalise and torment him to the point of no return, yet without granting him release.

He knew the enveloping heat of her mouth, the flickering torture of her tongue, the teasing touch of fingers which knew exactly what to do to drive him mad then stop him in midstream.

He tried closing his eyes against the sensations growing within him, and it proved to be a disastrous mistake. For during those seconds of desperate darkness she moved to straddle his hips, taking the full length of his pained hardness deep within her. His eyes flung open on a raw cry of panic, but already she was riding him, green eyes glittering wildly.

'No,' he groaned. But weakly. Pathetically.

'Yes,' she hissed back. 'Yes...'

His hands found her hips, and he should have heaved her from his body. Instead he gripped her flesh and urged her on to a stronger, faster rhythm. His own hips began to rise and fall, and it felt incredible.

God, but she was so hot in there. So hot. He could feel his own blood heating even further, racing along his veins like molten lava. The volcano of his desire would not be contained this time. Or controlled. It surged higher and higher with each drumbeat of his madly pounding heart, and then it was erupting, flooding into the already spasming heart of her womanhood, dredging raw groans from his parched and panting lungs.

When the climax had passed, he reached up to bring her down so that he could kiss her, wanting to feel the heat of her mouth as well.

He was startled to encounter the wetness of tears running into the corners. He didn't know what to say; could think of nothing but to cradle her close, to stroke her back and say whatever came to mind.

'Don't cry, darling. Please don't cry. God, but I can't bear it. Hush, sweetness. There's nothing to worry about. Nothing. As I said before, I'm a good guy. And I can see you're a good girl. We're good people. Hush, my loveliness. Hush. Go to sleep, there's a good girl. Yes, that's it. Go to sleep.'

They both went to sleep... eventually... though Luke took quite a while to come to terms with what had just happened. He hoped he was right. Hoped that she *was* a good girl. If not, he'd just done the stupidest damned thing he'd ever done in his whole life. Slept with a perfect stranger. *Without* protection. Then, to top it all off, he'd fallen in love with her...

'All finished, Mr St Clair.' The chair snapped upright and the nurse moved to unclip the paper bib around his neck.

Luke's black eyes blinked open to stare blankly into her smiling face. His gaze went to the clock on the wall. Eleven-fifteen. He'd been at the dentist over half an hour and he hadn't felt a thing! Unless one counted what had been going on within his head. And his heart.

An impotent rage simmered beneath the cool façade he presented to the dentist and his nurse as he thanked them and said goodbye, and then to the receptionist as he paid his bill. In cash.

'I hope you enjoy your stay here in Australia, Mr St Clair,' she said, reminding him that he still sounded like an American.

'I'm sure I will,' he returned, trying to keep the grim satisfaction out of his voice. 'Enjoy' was probably not the right word, but he had no doubt that this visit was going to be memorable. At last he had a name to put to his obsession. A name and a past. He would leave no stone unturned till he came face to face with the woman who'd haunted him all these months.

And when he did?

God only knew what he was going to do. Because *he* didn't.

'Would you mind if I took one of those old magazines with me?' he asked the receptionist. 'It has a picture in it of an old friend of mine.'

'Take it, by all means.' And me too if you like, her eyes seemed to be telling him.

Unfaithful bitch, he thought as he strode over to the corner table. They were probably all unfaithful bitches, all the beautiful women in this world.

He snatched up the magazine in question, not giving the girl a second glance as he stuffed it under his arm and strode angrily from the room.

CHAPTER THREE

His mother was waiting for him in the coffee-lounge, a cup of capuccino in front of her, a jam and cream doughnut to her left, a newspaper to her right and a plastic shopping bag at her feet. She shut the newspaper on Luke's approach and folded it, frowning up at him as he scraped out the chair and sat down.

'What's wrong with you now?' she said. 'Couldn't you get your tooth fixed?'

He resisted the urge to scowl. Five minutes he'd give her, then he'd be off in a taxi to the nearby airport, where he would rent a decent car. He needed his own wheels. And the privacy that went with them.

'There's nothing wrong with me,' he said. 'I'm fine. My tooth's fine. The weather's fine. Life's fine.'

'Then why are you still in such a foul mood?'

'Lord, what is it with you? Do you have some special mother's antenna that can pick up my mood at twenty paces? I've just walked in and sat down. How could you possibly gauge my mood? I hadn't even spoken when you made your instant judgement.'

'You were walking cranky,' came her simplistic but accurate observation.

41

He couldn't help it. He had to laugh. There was no hiding anything from his mother. Which reminded him. He slipped the magazine from under his arm onto a spare chair and thought of something to say to distract her.

'Tell me, Mum. Were you ever unfaithful to Dad?'

'Heavens to Betsy! What a question!'

'That's no answer. That's an evasion.'

'I needed a moment to catch my breath. Might I ask what's brought such a question on?'

'Well, you're a good-looking woman. From photographs I've seen when Dad married you forty-five years ago you were pretty stunning. Stunning women have temptation put in their way, whether they're married or not.'

Grace wondered which stunning married woman her son had been getting mixed up with, but tactfully refrained from asking. *This* time.

'I won't say I didn't have my offers,' she answered truthfully. 'And I won't say I wasn't tempted, once or twice. But I managed to stay faithful to your father. Technically speaking, that is.'

Luke blinked his shock at her. 'Technically speaking?' he repeated rather dazedly. 'What do you mean... "*technically* speaking"?'

'Well, I did let a man kiss me once for a few seconds longer than I should have.'

'Oh, is that all?'

'I thought it was pretty terrible of me at the time. But he was awfully good-looking. And very charming. I was flattered to death that he fancied me. He was only in his early thirties and I was a silly forty-one at the time, thinking I was over the hill and desperate for some attention. He gave me some.'

'And would have given you a whole lot more if you'd let him,' Luke said drily. 'Who was he, this Casanova?'

'No one you ever met. He was Danish, visiting Sydney one summer. Your father met him down the local pub and was silly enough to invite him home for supper one night.'

'And you let him kiss you that very same night?' Luke could not contain his surprise.

A small blush of guilt stained his mother's normally pale cheeks. 'As I said,' she muttered, 'he was very charming.'

'So how did it happen? And where was Dad, damn him?'

'Watching TV, as usual. Eric offered to help me with the washing-up, and he sort of cornered me against the kitchen sink. At first I was shocked. But when he started kissing me, I have to admit I liked it. Oh, I stopped him before things went too far, but after he left I thought about him a lot. I knew which hotel he was staying at—since he'd made a point of telling me—and I actually rang his room one day. But when he answered I panicked and hung up.'

'I see ...'

'Do you, Luke? I doubt it. I loved your father, and he was a good lover when he was younger. But time and familiarity can do dreadful things in the bedroom. Boredom sets in, and your father did work terribly hard. Most nights he was too tired. Our sex life had deteriorated to a quickie once or twice a month, and I was silly enough not to know what to do about it. So, of course, I was a ready victim for the likes of Eric, who really was a sleazebag of the first order.'

Luke frowned at his mother. 'You're not lying to me, are you, Mum? You didn't really go with him, did you?'

'Of course not! I went out and bought myself a sexy black nightie and started doing a few of those things I'd only ever read about in books before. Things really looked up after that.'

'Mum! I'm shocked,' he said, then grinned at her. 'You devil, you.'

She blushed some more, though she did look rather pleased with herself. He felt inordinately proud of her at that moment. She'd been handed temptation on a plate, when his dad had foolishly been neglecting her, but her essential goodness had come through in the end.

Luke's mouth thinned as he accepted that not all women were as strong, or as decent. Some were weak, self-centred creatures, who went out and took what they wanted, and to hell with the people they hurt in the process.

A waiter appeared by the table and asked Luke if he wanted to order. He declined, giving the excuse that his mouth still felt numb from the injection he'd had—which was true—but the real reason was that he could not stand to sit there any longer. He had places to go. Leads to follow. A woman to find.

'Would you mind if I loved you and left you, Mum?' he said as soon as the waiter had departed. 'While I was at the dentist's I remembered I'd promised Ray to look him up the next time I was home.'

'Ray? Ray who?'

'Ray Holland. He's a photographer.' Who I'm hoping and praying still lives and works in Sydney, he thought grimly.

'Never heard of him. There again, the only photographer friend of yours you ever talk about is Theo, and that's never very complimentary. I remember poor Theo had the hardest job talking you into going to the opening of his photographic exhibition last time you were home, and then the next morning he rang and complained that you'd disappeared ten minutes after you arrived!'

'Yeah, well, over the past few years poor Theo's work has gone from really good stuff down to the most pretentious crap. I thought if I stayed there any longer that night I might be tempted to tell the truth and offend him.'

'Where *did* you get to that night? You didn't come home, if I recall.'

'Come now, Mum! You don't really expect me to tell you, do you? I gave up reporting in when I turned eighteen.'

'Don't underestimate yourself, Luke. You were fifteen. The most difficult and rebellious boy God ever put breath into! I can see you haven't improved much either. You're still difficult.'

'What about rebellious?'

'"Rebellious" is not an adjective suited to a thirty-two-year-old bachelor. Let's just leave it at difficult.'

'Yes, let's,' Luke said, and stood up, sensing that his mother was about to deteriorate into emotional blackmail of some sort. She had that gleam in her eye which heralded that her female curiosity was far from satisfied.

Women could be quite ruthless when they really wanted to know something, he mused. If cool reason didn't work, they tried every trick in the book—from Chinese-water-torture-style demands, to sulky silences, to floods of tears.

Luke could bear just about all those methods except tears. They were the undoing of him every time.

'I must go, Mum. I have a lot to do today. And before you suggest it, no, I don't want you to drive me. I'm going to rent myself a car.'

'Will you be home for dinner this evening?' Grace asked archly.

'What are you cooking?'

She lifted her nose in a disdainful sniff. 'I have no intention of telling you if that's all that's bringing you home.'

'In that case you can surprise me. See you around seven, sweetie,' he said, distracting her with a peck on the cheek while he scooped the women's magazine up from the adjoining chair.

Grace watched her son stalk across the coffee-lounge, well aware of the hungry female eyes which turned to follow him. Her sigh held a weary resignation. That boy is up to no good, she thought, her own eyes zeroing in on the magazine curled up in his right hand.

And it's all to do with some woman, I'll warrant. A woman featured in that magazine he's been trying to hide. A married woman, no doubt, whom he met the last time he was home and whom he's off to meet again in secret.

Oh, Luke... Luke...

Grace shook her head unhappily. When was he going to learn that there was no future with a married woman? No future at all!

Luke paced up and down the living-room of Theo's apartment, impatiently waiting for his friend to come out of his darkroom.

He still could not believe his luck—or the ease with which he'd reached his objective! Within an hour of leaving his mother he'd been leaving the offices of the magazine with the address of Ray Holland in his hot little hands. Half an hour later Luke had been walking into the man's studio in Randwick, and once again his luck had been in—he'd caught the freelance photographer just before he had to leave. Luke had come to the point immediately.

A trendily dressed man in his early forties, Mr Holland had remembered the Cleary wedding very well, because he'd worked with the bride herself several times previously—her speciality having been modelling swimsuits and lingerie, both as a photographic and catwalk model.

He'd also heard on the grapevine that his 'darling Rachel'—Luke's teeth had ground when he'd called her that—had recently returned to modelling. Word around the photographic traps was that her scientist husband had died recently, and that financial difficulty had forced her to go back to work.

Luke had absorbed this last piece of news with ambivalent emotions. He hadn't been able to deny his momentary elation at finding out that the object of his obsession was now a widow, but the news that the husband had only died recently—meaning she'd still been well and truly married that night eighteen months ago—had revitalised his underlying bitterness towards her.

Unfaithful bitch, he'd raged inwardly while he'd taken down the name and address of the modelling agency she worked for.

The niggling suspicion that her much older husband might have been ailing at the time of her adultery had crossed his mind as he'd driven on to that agency. Such a circumstance might have mitigated her behaviour somewhat, if she'd gone about having her affair with some class and style, but there had been nothing of class or style in the way she'd been dressed that night—or the way she'd picked him up, or the way she'd slunk off afterwards while he'd been asleep.

That was one thing he would never forgive. Her running out on him the way she had—leaving him to worry and wonder, leaving him feeling a total fool and in torment for months, till a second blood test had assured him he wasn't about to die for his insanity in going to bed with such a creature.

He'd always wanted to meet her face to face, and see what it was about her that still haunted him so. But also to ask her why. Why she'd chosen him. Why she'd taken such a crazy risk. Why, why, why?

And now... Now he would have the opportunity to do just that... in two days' time. God, he could hardly wait!

'That's some smile, pal. It's sending shudders down my spine. What are you up to?'

Luke's dark eyes snapped up to find that Theo had emerged from the darkroom and was watching him closely. Theo had once been Luke's employer, in the early days. Now he was Luke's one remaining close friend in the Australian photographic world. Still a bachelor, he was an elegant-looking man in his late thirties who changed girlfriends as regularly as he did cameras and styles of photography.

Luke didn't like the way Theo slavishly followed the photographic fashion of the moment. He believed that that was not the road to success or personal satisfaction. But he liked the man, who was easy-going and great company. Unfortunately Theo could also sometimes be as intuitive as Luke's mother—something Luke had temporarily forgotten. His mind, after all, was rather preoccupied at that moment.

Luke casually wiped the darkly triumphant smile from his face, replacing it with an innocuously bland expression. 'I'm contemplating how you're going to react to my asking to borrow two of your cameras.'

Theo's blue eyes narrowed, suspicion in their intelligent depths. '*You* want to borrow *my* cameras?' he said, his voice sceptical in the extreme. 'That'd be a first.'

'True. But I've been thinking lately how bored to tears I am with photographing faces—especially in black and white. I've decided to try my hand at something different.'

'Such as what?' Theo walked across his living-room in the direction of his well-equipped kitchen. 'Care for a cup of coffee?'

Luke nodded, recognising the hunger pangs in his stomach for the first time that day. A glance at his watch showed him the reason why. Hell, it was after three, and he hadn't stopped for a bite to eat since breakfast!

It just showed what effect that witch could have on him, he thought blackly. She disturbed his equilibrium as no woman had ever done before. Splitting up with Tracy had left him feeling wretched and lonely for only a few short weeks. Not being able to find this Rachel, after spending one short night together, had shattered him for months, then haunted him for another year, spurring him on to indulge in a personal lifestyle which was basically abhorrent to him.

Neither was it working.

Being with other women didn't rid him of the memories of that night. It kept them alive by making him compare all the time. Yet no woman *could* compare—either with the physical feelings that that green-eyed alley-cat had initially evoked, or the emotional feelings she'd managed to engender later, once they had been alone together in that room.

'Penny for your thoughts,' Theo drawled as he slid a mug of coffee down the breakfast bar to where Luke had blindly propped himself up on a kitchen stool. Luke blinked a couple of times, then focused on his friend.

'They're worth a lot more than that,' he muttered, thinking of all the jobs he'd knocked back this last eighteen months. It was as well he'd become independently wealthy these past few years, or he'd have been stony broke by now.

'You're talking in riddles, man. Care to tell your old mate what's eating you up?'

'No. Not really.'

Theo nodded up and down, his expression accepting. 'Fair enough.'

Luke appreciated his friend's not pressing. Maybe he would tell him one day about this Rachel, depending on what happened on Wednesday. But there again...maybe not...

'So what cameras do you want to borrow?' Theo asked.

Luke shrugged, then grinned. 'Damned if I know. I'll have to put myself in your expert hands.'

Theo grinned back. 'Flattery will get you every-where. Well, first things first, what are you going to photograph?'

'Lots of beaches and bikinis.'

Theo's eyebrows shot up. 'Are we talking art-shots here, or some sort of Australiana promotion?'

'That depends,' Luke returned non-committally.

Theo's blue eyes twinkled. 'Ahh. Methinks I'm beginning to see what lies behind this unexpected career-change. And there I was thinking you were the only other man I knew to have escaped the tender trap. So! Might I enquire her name?'

'Who?' Luke drawled.

'The model you'll be using, man. What do you take me for—a fool? Now, give. Who is she? Do I know her, and why are you going to so much trouble to be with her?'

Luke decided he had nothing to lose by telling Theo her name. Who knew? Theo didn't do much fashion work any more, but he might still know her.

'Rachel Manning,' he said.

The agency had confirmed that she was working under her maiden name. They'd also confirmed that she was still specialising in swimwear and was free of bookings that week.

Luke's stomach had twisted into knots while they rang her on the spot and booked her for a shoot on the Wednesday and Thursday up on the Central Coast beaches, starting at Terrigal on the Wednesday, with an overnight stay at the Holiday Inn there that night.

Luke had known she wouldn't refuse—not if she needed money. He'd offered a top fee, feeling quite safe when he'd heard the agency inform her over the telephone that the photographer's name was Luke St Clair and that he was Australian, but had been working overseas.

'Don't recognise the name,' Theo muttered. 'There again, I never was good with names.'

'Not to worry,' Luke said, hating the way his heart was pounding just talking about her. He picked up his coffee-mug and sipped the now tepid drink.

Theo threw his friend a frustrated look. 'Well, aren't you going to tell me all about her?'

'Not at this stage.'

Theo's expressive eyebrows waggled up and down. 'Do I get to know all the sordid details afterwards?'

'For pity's sake, don't you have a sex life of your own?'

'Not for over a week now.'

Luke always laughed at Theo's crestfallen expression. 'A veritable drought,' he said drily.

'It is for me.'

'Maybe you should settle down, Theo. Find yourself a nice girl and get married.'

'Perish the thought.'

When Luke didn't say anything to this typical bachelor remark, Theo stared at him. Hard.

'You're not thinking of getting married, are you?' he said, almost accusingly. 'Damn it all, Luke, you haven't gone and fallen in love, have you?'

Luke didn't know what to say to either of those questions. Both distressed and confused him. His brain denied each in turn—the first as impossible, the second as highly improbable. Yet his heart leapt at both ideas.

Don't be a bloody fool, he told himself scathingly. The likelihood is that she's bad through and through. Bad and mad. You don't go giving your heart and your life to a woman like that!

'No,' he denied aloud. 'I'm not going to get married. And I haven't fallen in love.' What he *had* done, however, he rationalised brutally, was tumble headfirst into lust. A lust which hadn't had the opportunity to burn itself out. A lust which still simmered, waiting for the instigator to come back into his life.

Well, that instigator was going to come back this Wednesday, and Luke was going to do everything in his power to satisfy not only his curiosity about her, but everything else she'd managed to keep aroused in him for the past eighteen months.

CHAPTER FOUR

WEDNESDAY morning could not have dawned more perfect. At least weatherwise. A little crisp—since it was only the first week in September—but clear, with the promise of some real spring warmth later in the day.

The sun had crept over the ocean horizon at around six, quickly dispelling the grey pre-dawn light, its gleaming rays spearing through the Norfolk pines on the beachfront and hitting Luke's hotel room windows.

That had been nearly an hour ago, during which time he'd showered, shaved and dressed, before sitting down to eat the breakfast delivered to his room. Each mouthful had been accompanied by thoughts of *her*, already on her way up here, totally unaware of the true identity of Luke St Clair.

He had toyed with the idea of asking the agency to have her drive up the night before and stay here at the Holiday Inn with him, but he had dismissed it in the end as too dangerous. His intention was to catch her completely off guard, then sweep her into a day's supposed work before she could even think.

He had a plan of action which he hoped would work—a strategy which would put her in his secret power and possibly make her more open with him.

It would work too, if she felt guilty about what she'd done eighteen months ago.

And he suspected that she might.

Seven o'clock arrived—the time Luke had given the agency for her to meet him in the foyer of the hotel. Her instructions were to have his room paged if he wasn't there. Which he had no intention of being. Luke expected that it would take her a few minutes at least to decide to do this, even if she was on time. No one liked to rush things these days, and punctuality was not the virtue it used to be.

While he waited for the telephone call he wandered out onto the balcony of his hotel room. Leaning against the railing, he stared down, first at the magnificent turquoise swimming pool below, then out across the road to the beach and the sparkling blue sea beyond.

He'd chosen Terrigal because it was away from Sydney and he knew it quite well, having camped up here often with friends when he was in his late teens. All the local beaches were picturesque, and he knew that he would have no trouble finding some magnificent shots to photograph.

Above everything, Miss Rachel Manning was not to suspect that this was anything but a proper, professional photographic shoot. If she did, then all would be lost. No one liked to be fooled, or manipulated.

No one, Luke thought with a black bitterness.

The seconds began ticking away with agonising slowness. Five past seven came and went. Then ten past.

She was late.

A couple more minutes dragged by, but still no call came.

Luke was dismayed to find that he was beginning to feel more than a little agitated. He actually felt sick—sick with something like fear.

But fear of what?

Fear that she might not arrive at all? Or of finding out, when she did, that it had all been an illusion? What if he saw her again and felt...nothing? What if he found out that his obsession with her had all been a perverse fantasy of his mind?

The ring was shrill to his ears and he whirled around, staring back into the room and at the telephone sitting on the writing desk in the corner as if it were a cobra about to strike. Paralysed for a few moments, Luke listened to it ring and ring before lurching in onto the grey carpet and snatching the hated thing from its cradle.

'Yes?' he said sharply.

'Good morning, Mr St Clair,' the male desk-clerk said, in that smooth, unruffled voice which the best of hotel staff always possessed. 'Sorry to disturb you so early, sir, but there's a Miss Manning here who says her instructions were to have you paged when she arrived. She says she's sorry she's a little late, but there was an accident on the expressway.'

Luke's stomach churned some more. She was here...downstairs...waiting for him.

'Tell her I'll be down shortly,' he said in decidedly strangled tones.

'Very good, sir.'

Luke hung up, then dragged in several deep steadying breaths. This would never do. He couldn't let her frighten him. *She* was the one who was going to be frightened. At first. That was part of his revenge.

He checked his appearance in the long mirror hanging on the back of the bathroom door, approving of his choice of clothes. His tall, lean body looked well in jeans. Stonewashed grey this morning, matched to a simple white T-shirt and a lightweight charcoal-grey jacket which could be zipped up against the wind if necessary.

There was nothing about him to betray his wealth, except perhaps for his watch, which was a gold Rolex. Still, there were plenty of fake Rolexes in this world. Luke wasn't sure why he didn't want her to know how well-off he was, but he didn't. He almost regretted offering such an exorbitant fee, but without it she might not have come.

Steeling himself, he slipped the hotel room key into his pocket, smoothed his dark brown hair back from his face, covered his glittering black eyes with wrap-around sunglasses and left the room.

The lift carried him noiselessly down to the first floor, where he alighted, choosing to walk down the long sweeping staircase to the ground floor and give himself ample opportunity to survey the foyer and its occupants below as he did so.

She would not be expecting him to arrive that way. Neither would she be expecting *him*. Eighteen months ago she'd thought him an American, had believed he was only holidaying in Australia, unlikely to return and turn up in her life again.

But he *was* turning up, he thought with a grim satisfaction as he began a slow descent down the elegant staircase. And he had no intention of leaving again—not till he'd got what he wanted from her.

He walked slowly, his gaze searching the groupings of armchairs gathered in the centre of the foyer down below. They were all empty. His frown deepened as his eyes scanned first left and then right, towards the reception desk.

He didn't recognise her at first, for her back was to him and her hair was longer and straighter, and blonder. Almost white-blonde, in fact, hanging straight down her back. She was wearing black leggings and a black blazer-style jacket, with a canvas satchel slung over her shoulder. Black platform sandals made her look even taller than he remembered.

She was chatting away to the desk-clerk—probably the same one who had rung him. He was a good-looking young man and was smiling at her. Luke told himself that it wasn't jealousy which jabbed at his heart, merely cynicism. She was still good at picking up members of the opposite sex, it seemed.

No doubt now, being a merry widow, she was making up for lost time. There would no longer be any need for subterfuge with her one-night stands—or deceit. She could have whatever man she fancied, whenever she fancied.

Luke's loins leapt at the thought, assuaging his earlier fear that he might not still want her.

The clerk must have spotted him coming down the stairs and said something to her, for she turned to look up at him.

His breath caught in his throat and he hesitated momentarily. For, although he knew it was the same woman—impossible to mistake those eyes—there was nothing of the sultry or seductive about the clear-skinned, clear-eyed face which tipped back to stare up at him. She was all natural beauty, fresh and innocent-looking, in a simple white blouse which buttoned right up to the neck. A sweetie, not a siren. A virgin, not a vamp.

Luke almost laughed at this last thought, his stupidity firing his fury and his feet forward. She was no virgin, this chameleon. No sweetie either. She was twenty-six years old, and a cool, calculating witch of a woman.

He revelled in the way her high, wide forehead began to crease into a frown as she continued to survey his measured descent. No doubt with his sunglasses firmly in place she couldn't be sure of his identity, but something was definitely teasing her brain. And her memory.

Meanwhile he soaked her in. Every gorgeous inch of her. Damn, but she was beautiful. So beautiful that he already ached with longing to possess her just one more time. No, once would not be enough. He had to have her more than that. He had to have till he could not bear to do it one more time.

Maybe then he would be at peace.

Maybe then he would stop fantasising that he was in love with her.

He chose the perfect moment to remove his sunglasses, having schooled his face into a superbly bland expression, masking his feelings behind a façade so cool and so casual that she would surely have to doubt his own recognition of her.

The glasses swept aside, he strode across the tiled foyer floor, disarming her totally by smiling politely then reaching out his hand as he drew near. 'Miss Manning, I presume?'

Her obvious shock disintegrated into confusion, her stunned gaze going from his face to his outstretched hand and to his face again. Clearly she had no practice at facing a one-night stand who failed to recognise her. And clearly she was very disconcerted.

To give her credit, she swiftly pulled herself together, placing a brave but betrayingly shaky hand in his for a few brief moments before dredging up a polite smile of her own from somewhere.

'That's correct,' she said, her voice crisp and rather strained, with not a trace of the huskily sexy tones she'd used on him that night. 'And you're Mr St Clair?'

'The one and only,' he drawled.

'But...but the agency said you were an Australian photographer.'

'And so I am. The accent is just a relic of my living and working in LA for ten years.'

'Oh. Oh, I see...'

No, you don't, you deceiving witch. You can't see at all! But *he* could. Could see perfectly how relieved she was to find that he didn't recognise her. She'd gone almost as white as her hair for a moment, but now the colour was flooding back into her cheeks—those gorgeous cheeks and gorgeous cheekbones and gorgeous everything else!

'I come home to Sydney for a visit every now and then,' he went on, silkily putting her mind at ease some more. 'This time I decided to combine my holiday with a little work. Last time I came home I did far too much partying and spent most of the time totally hungover. You don't mind if I call you Rachel, do you? And you must learn to call me Luke. First names are much more relaxing than Miss and Mr, don't you think?'

'I suppose so.'

Her wariness was gradually dissolving, although not entirely gone yet. A certain tension remained. She wasn't comfortable with him or the situation, that much was evident.

'Ready to start work?' he asked abruptly, sliding his sunglasses back into place over his eyes. The opaque lenses and wrap-around style gave him the opportunity to study her and her reactions closely without her being too aware of it.

'What? Oh . . . oh, yes—yes, I guess so.'

There was no doubting that she was still highly agitated. He wasn't sure if he liked that or not. On-going agitation did not fit in with the image of her he'd carried around all these months, or of how he'd imagined she'd react to his supposedly not recognising her.

After the initial shock, he'd expected her to quickly take his reappearance in her life in her stride. Now that she was a widow, he was even hoping she'd be flirtatious with him.

Such was not the case. She was stiff and silent, her lovely green eyes clouded with worry.

'Where have you parked your car?' he asked, annoyed with himself for feeling guilt over what he was doing. Clearly the guilt was all on her part, which was as it should be. But he did wish she'd stop flicking him those anxious and startled glances, as though she still could not believe who Luke St Clair had turned out to be.

'In the street,' she said, nodding towards the revolving glass door. 'Outside.'

'Do you need anything out of it for the day?'

'No, not really. I have all my make-up and hair things in here.'

'In that case I suggest you drive your car up to the hotel entrance and I'll arrange to have it parked downstairs, in the hotel car park. You are staying here tonight, after all.'

The momentary terror which flashed into her face absolutely floored him. 'Well, I... Well, actually, I don't think... I mean,' she stumbled and bumbled. 'I... I might have to go home tonight,' she finished up, all flushed and flustered. 'I can always drive up again in the morning.'

Luke stared at her from behind his glasses. What in hell was going on here? Why was she so frightened of him? Or, more to the point, of staying at the same hotel with him?

Could it be that she still wanted him, as he still wanted her, but that she didn't *want* to want him? Could it be that she was afraid to put herself into a potentially intimate situation with him, lest she surrender to the temptation to do what she'd done once before?

But why would that frighten her? he puzzled, at the same trying to contain his excitement that this deduction might be right.

The obvious answer to his question brought a sickening jolt to his stomach. There had to be another man on the scene. If not a husband then a fiancé, or a boyfriend, or a lover. Maybe, once again, she was not free to dally with whomever she fancied.

Hell, he hadn't thought of that. Yet he should have. A woman like her would not be alone for long.

'And where is home, exactly?' he asked curtly.

'Caringbah.'

Caringbah was a Sydney suburb even more south than his mother's own Monterey.

'But that's a good two hours' drive,' he argued. 'Surely the boyfriend can do without you for one night?' he added, trying not to sound as blackly jealous as he was feeling.

'Boyfriend?' she repeated blankly, and Luke's heart soared.

There was no boyfriend. No boyfriend and no lover and no fiancé. He was sure of it!

'I was trying to think of the reason why you'd have to go home,' he said, thrown back to the original puzzle. Why *was* she afraid of him?

'My... my mother-in-law hasn't been well,' she explained, if reluctantly. 'I've been a little worried about leaving her for the night.'

'You live alone with your mother-in-law?'

Her hesitation to answer inflamed his curiosity further. 'Yes,' she said at last. 'Yes, I do. I ... I'm a widow, you see,' she admitted tautly.

'Ahh...' He didn't really see, of course. And it was killing him. 'Well, perhaps you could give her a call later in the day and put your mind to rest. I'm sure she wouldn't want you driving all the way back home through Sydney in peak hour traffic, only to have to turn round and come back the next morning.'

'No—no, I suppose not.'

'That's settled, then. You can ring her after we've finished for the day. Now, off you go and get your car while I speak to the parking attendant.'

He watched her walk away, watched the way the breeze blew her long fair hair once she'd made it through the revolving door. Her right hand lifted to hold it back from her face, and when she glanced back over her shoulder at him he found himself caught up in her stunning beauty once more.

Yet it was such a different beauty this time—her lovely face free of make-up, her lush breasts no longer put on blatant display, her sexuality and sensuality much more subtle.

The effect on Luke was twice as strong.

He stood there, staring at her, every muscle in his body stiff with instant tension. She frowned back for a few seconds, then turned and strode off with long, elegant strides. Luke had to almost literally drag his eyes away from her. Damn, but he wanted her more than ever. Would *die* if he didn't spend this coming night with her.

Yet achieving that end this time would not be as easy as he'd hoped it would be. She meant to resist him, that was clear. Though the reason was not. He tried reassuring himself that she still found him physically attractive. She had once, and most women did.

So there had to be other factors involved—factors hidden from him but which hopefully might become clearer as the day wore on.

When she stepped out of her small white sedan a couple of minutes later, she too was wearing sunglasses, which irritated Luke. Now he couldn't see what she was thinking, or feeling. Still, she would have to take them off for the shoot. He vowed to slip in a few pointed questions whenever he had her at his visual mercy.

'Where's *your* gear?' she asked.

'In my car.'

'Which is?'

'Down where your car is heading. There's a door over here,' he went on, taking her nearest arm in a firm grip. 'This way...'

Her instant disengaging of his arm held a distressed fluster which startled then infuriated him.

'Sorry,' he bit out. 'I was only trying to help. I didn't realise you were one of those women who don't like to be touched.'

God, but did he have to sound so sarcastic, so bloody cynical?

'Sorry again,' he said quickly. 'That sounded rotten, and I didn't mean it to.' Which was so true. Hell, the last thing he wanted was to tip her off that he recognised her.

'No, *I'm* sorry,' she said with a shuddering sigh. 'I was being super-touchy. Look, the thing is I had this rather unfortunate experience with a male photographer a while back, and I've become a little gun-shy of being alone with them ever since.'

Luke was astonished by his immediate and fierce fury against the creep. 'What happened? My God, he didn't assault you, did he?'

'No, no, it didn't go that far,' she hastened to explain. 'But the man's attentions were...unwanted. I found the whole thing most distasteful.'

'You've nothing to fear from me, Rachel,' he assured her, and for the life of him he almost meant it! Good God, what was it about this woman that made him want to protect her at the same time as just wanting her? 'I've never had to force myself on a woman in my life,' he muttered, 'and I can't see myself starting now.'

A small rueful smile tugged at her lovely mouth. 'No,' she said softly. 'No, I can appreciate that.'

Luke slanted her a long glance, then took her arm again. This time she did not resist him.

It came to him then that she might not resist him tonight either, if he played his cards right. Her earlier fear had not been of him, but of that other fool, who'd been stupid enough to play rough with her. If Luke had learnt one thing from his other experience, it was that darling Rachel liked to take the lead in matters of sex and seduction. She liked doing the choosing and she preferred being on top, quite literally.

An electric current charged along Luke's veins as he struggled to suppress the hot memory of what she'd looked like that night—her back arched, her head thrown back, her lips parted.

But he failed miserably.

It took all of his control to lead her quietly downstairs to the underground car park and over to his rented white Futura. He would much rather have dragged her over to a dark corner and kissed her with all the mad desire already bubbling up inside him.

Patience, Luke, he kept telling himself. Patience. Tonight will come, and when it does...

He clenched his teeth hard in his jaw to stop the groan from escaping. Today was going to be hell. But a hell he had to endure. She simply was not going to be rushed.

Besides, he had more things to satisfy than his damned body. He still didn't have any answers to all those other questions which had plagued him this past eighteen months.

Yes, patience, he repeated to himself. That was the key. All things came to those who waited. Rachel had come, and so would all the other answers. All he had to do was wait.

CHAPTER FIVE

'WHAT swimsuit company are you doing these shots for?' she asked as he drove up the ramp of the underground car park and out into the sunshine.

Luke had been waiting for that question, and was glad that he'd worked out a good cover story.

'Actually, they're not for a swimsuit company. They're for the Central Coast Tourist Bureau, for a brochure they're producing. They only wanted scenic shots at first, but I convinced them that a gorgeous Australian blonde in a bikini would give their beaches some added appeal and impetus.'

Luke turned the car to the left and headed for the Skillion—a nearby headland which would make a good backdrop for some photos.

She slanted him a frowning glance. 'How come you chose me? I haven't been doing much work of late.'

'Yes, so the agency told me.' Luke thought he was being superbly casual, considering the state of his insides. 'You were recommended to me by an acquaintance. Ray Holland.'

Her mouth broke into a soft smile. 'Dear Ray. Now, there's a really nice man.'

'He says he did your wedding photographs.'

The smile faded. 'Yes, that's right,' she said stiffly, and fell silent.

Luke decided not to pursue the topic at this early stage, for fear of making her clam up entirely. He swung the car off Terrigal Drive onto the side road which led past the bay called the Haven and round to the base of the Skillion. Even at this early hour there were a couple walking hand in hand up the steep grassy incline which led up to the lookout and the abrupt drop beyond.

Luke noticed with a frown that a fence had been built since he'd last been up there some years back— no doubt as a guard against accidents. Anyone wanting to commit suicide would hardly have let a fairly low fence deter them. Still, the wooden and wire construction would not enhance any close-ups.

'If you're thinking of taking some shots of me up there,' Rachel said, glancing up at the unprotected clifftop, 'it'll be very windy.'

Luke frowned as he parked, nose frontwards, in a small cleared area to the left of the Skillion. He'd already dismissed the idea because of the fence, anyway.

'What about down there?' he suggested, pointing through the windscreen at the tiny rocky cove which lay straight ahead. 'I could still get the cliff in the background if I angled things right. What do you think?'

'I think that would be much better. Not as uncomfortable or as cold either. By the way, where am I supposed to change into the swimsuits?'

Luke almost swore. He hadn't thought of that. 'You'll have to do it in the back of the car,' he said. 'Sorry, I'm a bit out of practice at organising this type of shoot. Most of my photography these days is done inside.'

'And what type of photography is that?' she asked, her dry tone accompanied by a suspicious look.

Luke laughed. 'No, not that type. I specialise in portraiture.'

'And you make a good living from that?'

'I've done quite well out of it, actually.' Luke despised himself for suddenly wanting to brag. Where had his idea gone about her not knowing that he was well-off? Luke appreciated that his male ego could work against him at times, but the last thing he wanted was for Rachel to pay attention to him because she thought he was filthy rich.

He wished he knew what the circumstances of her marriage had been. How old her husband had actually been, and whether he had been wealthy to begin with. It would be naïve of him to discount her being a gold-digger, or even to assume that she *hadn't* come out of her marriage with the proverbial pot of gold.

She might not have come back to work out of financial difficulty at all. She might have merely wanted to put herself back into circulation. Hard to meet prospective lovers and husbands if one stayed at home with one's mother-in-law.

'Tell me, Luke, are you famous or something?' she asked. 'The agency implied you were very well known worldwide, but I thought they might be exaggerating. They have a tendency to do that sometimes.'

'I'm quite well known in California,' he admitted carefully, 'but I doubt too many people in Australia would even recognise my name.'

'I certainly didn't,' she said, and there was a wry note in the words.

'I wouldn't have expected you to. Now, why don't you slip into the back seat while I get the cameras and bikinis out of the boot?'

'Only bikinis?'

'You have some objection to that?'

'No. I just... I just...'

'Just what?'

'Nothing,' she muttered. 'I guess I've got out of the habit of freezing to death. This is my first outdoor assignment since coming back to modelling.'

'You can wear your jacket till I'm ready to shoot. Hopefully, when we get to the beaches, there'll be proper dressing-rooms for you to change in.'

'Which one do you want me to wear first?' she asked when he handed the costumes through the back window a couple of minutes later.

Luke had gone to a local boutique when he'd arrived the previous afternoon, and had bought several assorted bikinis in the size the agency had given him. All were colourful and depressingly minute, he recalled ruefully.

'Makes no difference,' he returned, truthfully enough. Luke suspected that he was in trouble no matter which one she wore. 'Whatever one you fancy.'

'Stand with your back against the window,' she ordered. 'And no peeking!'

Luke had to work hard to keep a straight face as he did as he was told. Good God, there wasn't an inch of her that he hadn't seen—and at very close hand.

Still, the knowledge that she was taking off her clothes right behind him was tantalising in the extreme. He tried to keep his mind off the fact, aware of the discomfort that being turned on would cause him.

And he was marginally successful till the moment she climbed out of the car and that damned black jacket of hers flapped wide open for a few seconds.

Luke grimaced.

God, her body was even better! Her breasts looked fuller, and infinitely more lush, squashed as they were into the colourful half-cup bra. He decided that she must have put on a little weight, because her hips seemed curvier and her stomach rounder. The only things which looked exactly the same were her legs—those long, endless legs, whose firm honey-coloured thighs made him think of things that a man in tight jeans should never have thought of for more than a moment.

Luke suppressed a tortured groan and wrenched his eyes away, pretending to adjust the distance and light meters on the two cameras hanging around his neck.

Actually, Theo had already set them perfectly for him, giving him easy instructions for the odd possible adjustment and at the same time telling him that even a fool couldn't make a mistake taking photographs with his two beauties.

Luke began to appreciate that he *was* a fool, to think he could look at this particular woman all day, dressed in next to nothing, and not become a quivering wreck. His plan to question her at the same time, cleverly extracting the information he wanted before setting about as callous and calculating a seduction as she had perpetrated on him, now seemed ludicrous. He would be lucky if he was bloody *sane* by the end of *this* day!

'Having trouble with the camera?' she asked, with a seemingly ingenuous innocence.

'Just a little.' Luke stopped fiddling with the Nikon and looked up again. Thank God the blazer was now firmly wrapped around her, and thank God he could keep his sunglasses on. His eyes had a habit of betraying him when he wanted a woman. They sort of blazed away, with pinpoints of light glittering wildly within their darkened depths.

Or so he'd been told.

In a way, he was sorry she'd had to take her sunglasses off, for those big, beautiful green eyes gazing unguardedly at him were almost as disturbing as her unclad body.

'Both these cameras belong to a friend of mine,' he explained rather sharply. 'All my equipment is still in America.' Except the equipment I *had* to bring with me, he thought with rueful savagery. Pity I couldn't have left some of that behind as well!

Damn, but he hated being a man sometimes. Women had by far the best deal sexually. They could hide how they felt, or fake it splendidly, and no one was any the wiser. Whereas men's responses were brutally on display for all the world to see.

Gritting his teeth, he willed his body to a modicum of comfort and strode over to find the best way down to the rocky cove. There were several pathways between the rocks, which didn't look all that dangerous till he began following one and his foot slipped on a patch of loose gravelly dirt.

'Watch your step,' he ordered, glancing back up at her as she moved to follow him down the path he'd chosen. 'It's a bit slippery in parts, and we wouldn't want you falling and hurting yourself.'

He might have taken her hand and helped her down, but he suspected that that was not a good idea—either for his immediate peace of mind or the future success of his mission. After what had happened earlier, back in the hotel, he didn't think it was a good idea to touch her at all...till the moment was right.

The photograph session down on the rocks went surprisingly well—Luke managing temporarily to put his desire aside by concentrating on making each shot the very best he could take. It was an automatic response to what had been his profession for many years. A pride thing, really. If he was going to take photographs, he was going to take damned good ones. Unfortunately, to do so, he had to take his sunglasses off, for it really was impossible with them on. Sunglasses distorted one's sense of light and colour.

Fifteen minutes into the shoot, Luke realised that Rachel Manning was an exceptionally good model. A gem, in fact. Not only did the camera love her, she was also a true professional. She adopted the exact poses he was looking for with little prompting, her attitude and expression immediately echoing whatever image he wanted. Natural. Athletic. Girl-next-door. Bright and breezy. Dreamy.

It was the dreamy one that began his undoing. The way she arched her spine and dropped her head back, closing her eyes and smiling—so softly, and yet so...so...

'Now sexy,' he ordered, his voice thick and husky. 'Give me sexy.'

She shot him a startled glance before turning her eyes away and immediately giving him exactly what he'd stupidly asked for.

She lay back down on the smooth grey rock she'd been sitting on, her arms lifting up over her head to splay the long fair strands out with her fingers. Her back arched a little away from the rock and she bent her left knee slightly. It was then that she turned towards the camera, half opened her eyes and parted her lips in a pose so provocatively sensual that Luke's blood went from zero to boiling point in two seconds flat.

He swore under his breath and pressed his eye harder against the viewfinder, which didn't improve things at all. His trembling finger moved and the camera clicked, not once but several times, before he got a hold of himself.

'That's great,' he complimented curtly. 'But that's enough for here. We'll move on to another spot. I'll just walk up the Skillion and get some postcard-style shots of the surrounding area before we do. You can pop yourself back into the car and warm up. Change costumes while you're waiting, if you like.'

Luke was scrambling back up the path when he heard her cry out. It was not a loud cry, but his heart leapt with alarm at the pained sound, and he whipped around to find her still sitting on the edge of the rock and frowning down at the small rock pool in which her feet were resting.

Thoughts of the deadly blue ringed octopus which could lurk in such pools had the blood draining from Luke's face. 'What is it?' he called out. 'You haven't been bitten, have you?'

Had his panic sounded in his voice? It must have, for her eyes widened on him as though she was thoroughly taken aback by his burst of fierce concern. As was Luke. He hadn't realised till that moment how much she meant to him—however perverse that meaning was.

'No,' she said, peering down into the pool. 'Some fool's been drinking down here and smashed a beer bottle against this rock. This pool's full of broken glass and I think I just stood on a bit. Don't worry, it's only a little piece by the feel of things. I'll just pull it out and wash my foot in the salt water. That should kill any germs.'

'No, don't touch it!' he said sharply. 'I'll come and look and make sure that's all it is.'

Luke hurried back down the path and over to where she was still looking at him with a bewildered expression on her lovely face. 'Truly, there's no need to fuss,' she said. 'I'm perfectly all right.'

'I'll be the judge of that,' Luke said, sitting down beside her on the rock and lifting her dripping feet gently up into his lap. 'Better to be safe than sorry,' he muttered.

She was right, however. It *was* a piece of broken beer bottle, speared right in the middle of the big toe of her left foot.

'Does it hurt much?' he asked her as he examined it to see if there was enough sticking out for him to pull it out with his fingers, turning her foot this way and that to catch the sunlight against the glass.

'N-no.'

Her stammering was so unlike her cool self that he snapped his eyes up, thinking that she might have gone into some kind of shock.

But it wasn't shock he saw in her face. It was tension. A blindingly electric sexual tension.

His fingers grew hotly aware of the frozen stillness in the foot he was holding, then of the sudden pounding of his own heart. The temptation to slide a hand up her calf was enormous.

'There's enough glass sticking out for me to pull it out without tweezers,' he said, finding some satisfaction in the fact that his voice remained cool and controlled.

'Do it, then,' she said thickly.

He did, and for a split-second there was nothing to show where it had been. But then the blood began to ooze from her skin, and before Luke could appreciate what he was doing he'd lifted her foot and bent his mouth at the same time, pressing his lips against the cut and sucking it clean.

The primitive intimacy of his instinctive action was slow to sink in, but when it did Luke's stomach contracted fiercely. He raised his head to look at her, and found that she was staring at him with wide green eyes, her lips parting softly under her fast, shallow breathing.

Seeing her arousal did terrible things to Luke. He'd spent eighteen months fantasising about having her in his sexual power. Now that he did, all hell broke loose.

That old dark fury welled up within him, and it was with deliberately wicked intent that he straightened and lifted her foot higher, then higher, till she was tipped back against the gentle incline of the rock. This time he took her whole toe into his mouth.

He sucked on it slowly, revelling in the way her eyes gradually went from round frightened orbs to narrow slits of desire, their green colour darkening to a smoky grey, her lips falling further apart under the ragged panting sounds that were coming from her lips.

Luke stared at those lips, remembering how they had felt when she'd done the same to his desire-filled flesh, and knowing that he would not rest till he thrilled to that experience again. But at *his* behest this time—not hers. He wanted her to be at *his* mercy, not the other way around.

Hearing distant laughter reminded him starkly of where they were, in full view of anyone and everyone walking up the Skillion. Hardly the place for a proper seduction.

The realisation that *she* was beyond hearing or seeing anything brought a swift jab of savage satisfaction. It was so different from his previous experience with her, where in the end she'd taken control of the lovemaking while he'd been totally off the planet—oblivious to everything but his own pleasure. Luke sensed that the boot was on the other foot at this moment, so to speak.

When he abruptly plucked her toe from his mouth she gasped, her stunned eyes showing him that she could hardly believe she'd allowed herself to get so carried away. Luke decided to salvage her pride temporarily, by pretending that he hadn't even noticed her sexual response to his ministrations and giving all his attention to her cut toe and not to her anguished face.

'That seems to have stopped the bleeding,' he said off-handedly. 'But we wouldn't want any dirt getting in there, so I'll carry you up to the car.'

'No!' she immediately blurted out, whereat he lifted a mock-innocent gaze.

'But why not? I assure you I can manage. I'm stronger than I look.'

'I never said you didn't look strong,' she bit out. 'But I prefer to go under my own steam, thank you. I . . . I'll hop.'

'Suit yourself.' When Luke felt the beginnings of a darkly smug smile tug at his mouth, he stood up quickly and turned away.

But his thoughts stayed with her. I've got you where I want you now, Miss Rachel Manning. You've just shown me that the cool, professional persona you've been projecting today is just a sham. Underneath you're still the same woman who picked me up that night. Your sexuality still simmers just beneath the surface, ready to be tapped by any man who has the right tools.

And that man is going to be me tonight, lady, Luke vowed as he made his way to the car. And for as many nights as it will take to rid you from my body and my mind! For I can't go on as I've been going on. I have to free myself of you ... or make you mine forever.

Luke ground to a halt, disturbed by this last tacked-on thought. He recalled Theo's accusation that he had fallen in love and that he wanted to get married.

Luke whirled to glare at the woman who was the root cause of all his confusion, only to melt at the sight of her struggling to hop between the rocks. Furious with himself, and her, he covered the ground which separated them with angry strides, and before she could do more than squeal he swept her up into his arms.

'If there's one thing I can't stand,' he growled, 'it's a woman who won't ask a man for help when she needs it. You need me, Rachel. Why don't you just admit it?'

Their eyes locked—his blazing with frustration and hers bewildered. They searched his face, as though looking for something, till finally her chin tilted up proudly and her eyes cleared as she nodded slowly up and down.

'All right, Luke,' she said, her voice husky, yet quite composed. 'I'll admit it. I need you.'

A tremor raced through him, and he knew that once again the control had somehow slipped from his hands to hers.

Damn it all, he raged privately. Damn it!

The struggle to regroup his emotions was not easy. But he managed it, a cool smile masking any lingering exasperation.

'I'm glad to hear that, Rachel,' he said smoothly. 'A man likes to be needed. It makes him feel good. Now, let's get you up to the car and find a Bandaid,' he went on, adopting a very businesslike attitude. 'We have a long day ahead of us and a lot of work to be done.'

CHAPTER SIX

LUKE made it through the day.

Just.

His pride and ego came to the rescue—to a degree. Theo had magnanimously offered to develop all the films when he returned the cameras, so Luke's aversion to making a fool of himself—personally and photographically speaking—gave him the motivation to focus on what he was doing.

His aversion to making a fool of himself with women in general—and Rachel Manning in particular—also kept him safe during the moments when he wasn't taking photographs.

Not that he allowed too many of those. He swept her from Terrigal Beach straight to Wamberal, from there north to Forrester's Beach then on to Shelley's. A quick takeaway lunch at the Entrance was followed by further lengthy and quite gruelling sessions around the Entrance area and the surrounding lakes.

Conversation was kept to a minimum and was strictly professionally based. Luke had abandoned any idea of trying to worm out the personal and private details of Rachel's life and marriage while photographing her semi-naked.

He knew that it would be a waste of time and potentially hazardous to his razor-edge composure.

He ruefully resolved to wait till dinner that night, when she would be fully dressed and hopefully under the influence of some relaxing glasses of wine.

Not that he expected her to tell him much, even then.

Rachel Manning was a cool customer all right—a mysterious and enigmatic creature who was really impossible to manipulate. Luke had the awful feeling that she was playing with him, like a cat with a mouse. He would catch her looking intently at him sometimes, as though trying to fathom what she would do with him in the end. Put him out of his misery? Or just leave him dangling...?

By the time the sun began to set and the air to cool Luke was utterly exhausted—physically, mentally and emotionally. He was also on his last roll of film.

'Let's call it a day,' he said abruptly.

'You don't want to try for any sunset shots?'

He shot her a sharp look. Who did she think she was kidding? She had to be exhausted too, yet she was wanting to prolong things further? 'No,' he bit out. 'I'm too tired. You must be too. Let's get back to the hotel. I could do with a long hot bath and a stiff drink.'

Her shrug seemed indifferent, but Luke gained the impression of a real reluctance for the evening to begin. He also thought he detected a glimmer of something like fear in her eyes.

His irritation as he strode back to the car knew no bounds. He wished she'd make up her damned mind what she wanted from him. He wished he could make up his mind what he wanted from her.

He also wished he could make up his mind what he believed about her. He'd labelled her an adulterous whore in his mind.

Now he wasn't so sure.

Which wasn't anything new. When had he ever been sure of her, or of anything she did? She was full of mysteries and contradictions, and the most aggravating changes of character.

The question was...who was the real Rachel Manning? What was she? Where had she come from and where was she going to?

Luke knew that he had to have some answers to those questions before he dared do anything sexual with her again—before he dared become any more emotionally involved.

And he *was* emotionally involved with her. That was one thing he was sure of. Exactly what that emotion was eluded him. Love, or hate. Lust, or simply fury. All he knew was that she was not going to play him for a fool again. He wanted answers and he wanted her. And he aimed to get everything he wanted this time—no matter what.

Hell, he would get her blind drunk if he had to!

All was fair in love and war. And this, Luke vowed darkly, was war! She wasn't going to get away scot-free this time. No, sirree. He'd waited eighteen interminable months for this opportunity, and he wasn't going to let it slip away from him.

* * *

By seven twenty-five that evening Luke was ready, refreshed and reasonably relaxed. Three Scotches in a row did rather have that effect on one.

He'd arranged to collect Madam Manning from her room at seven-thirty and take her down to dinner, having booked an intimate little corner table for two at the Norfolk Terrace Restaurant on the first floor.

At seven twenty-six he gave his appearance a last checkover, telling himself that he looked quite dashing in charcoal-grey trousers, black silk shirt and a pale grey sports jacket. A little gel made his dark brown hair look almost black in the night light, the slicked-back style suiting his strongly boned face and bringing attention to his best feature—his eyes.

They gleamed back at him in the mirror, his bitter resolve bringing a dangerously ruthless edge to the smile that found its way to his mouth.

'Let's go, handsome.' He lifted a sardonic eyebrow at himself in the mirror. 'And remember, this is the moment you've been waiting for. Don't stuff it up.'

Madam's room was on the same floor but at the opposite end of the long corridor. He hadn't wanted to be too obvious by asking for adjoining rooms.

Luke felt some resurgence of nerves during the longish walk down to her room, but remained in firm control of them. He found it irritating, however, to have to knock twice before she opened the door.

'Sorry to keep you waiting,' she said briskly. 'I was on the telephone. I'll just get my purse.'

She left the door open while she did so, showing Luke a carbon copy of his own room. There might have been some minutely different details, but the blue and yellow colour-scheme was pretty much identical—the warm-wooded colonial furnishings very comfy, and pleasing to the eye.

It was classy accommodation with classy accoutrements. Luke was no stranger to five-star hotels all over the world, and this was as good as any he'd stayed in.

She walked back towards him, looking stunning and elegant in a silky green trouser-suit which had wide bottoms and a long flowing jacket with long sleeves and buttons right up to the neck. Despite the modesty of her clothes and the subtlety of her make-up, she looked incredibly sexy as she moved. Her loosely curled blonde hair swung about her face and shoulders. Her breasts—which might or might not have been braless—swayed sensuously beneath her top, riveting Luke's eyes.

He could have sworn her nipples peaked as he stared at them, but she didn't miss a beat as she swished out of the room, shutting the door behind her.

'Did you have that long hot bath you wanted?' she asked, her manner so cool that he might have imagined his staring had affected her in any way.

Except that Luke was gradually getting used to the fact that Miss Rachel Manning had two barometers. Her brain and her body. She could say one thing, he was beginning to appreciate, and feel quite another.

Luke determined to look past her words in future, to her more revealing body language. Yes, a quick glance revealed that her nipples very definitely had hardened. He could see them clearly outlined against the thin silk. He wasn't sure if he was contemptuous of her sexual vulnerability to such a small stimulus as a look, or excited by it.

Both, probably.

'Sure did,' he drawled. 'And a good stiff drink as well. And how did *you* fill in the last two hours?'

She slipped the key into her purse, her expression blandly pleasant. 'Oh, I soaked in a tub as well, then wickedly indulged in several cups of coffee while watching my favourite game-shows on television.'

'You're a caffeine addict, are you?' he remarked as they walked together down the corridor towards the lifts.

'Decidedly. A game-show addict as well.'

'Would that we all had such harmless addictions,' he murmured drily.

'Oh? And to what are you addicted, Luke St Clair?'

They had stopped at the twin lifts and she'd turned to face him, her expression seemingly ingenuous and curious. He eyed her closely in return while wondering what game she'd decided to play with him tonight. She appeared bent on a more leisurely seduction this time, confident in the power of her physical attraction and knowing full well that she only had to crook her finger at most men and they would come running. It would never have crossed her mind that he might knock her back.

Luke almost wished he could, but masochism had never been one of his fetishes.

'Where would you like me to begin?' he said nonchalantly.

'At the beginning might be a good start. I'd like to know what you were like as a little boy. Where did you grow up? How did you get into photography?'

He was startled, and showed it. Damn, she was doing it again—taking further control and reversing more roles. *He* should have been the one asking *her* questions, not the other way round.

'Why do you want to know?' he asked, punching the 'down' button on the wall between the twin lift-wells.

Her shrug was superbly nonchalant. 'We have to talk about something over dinner, don't we? I've never known a man who didn't like talking about himself.'

'Ouch,' he said lightly, though underneath he was piqued by her answer. There he'd been, suddenly thinking she was interested in Luke St Clair the man, not just Luke St Clair the male body. More fool him. 'You don't seem to have a high opinion of the male gender,' he added blithely.

'No,' she returned wryly. 'I can't say I'm overly impressed in general.'

This judgemental reply sparked a sharp response from Luke. Who in hell did she think she was—a saint?

'I'm not in the business of impressing women,' he said rather coldly. 'As far as I'm concerned they can take me or leave me.'

'I wasn't talking about you, Luke,' she denied. 'But from the sounds of things you're not all that impressed with the female gender in general either.'

His slow, sexually knowing smile was designed to melt even the iciest of women. 'You shouldn't take my cynicism personally, Rachel,' he said, in a low, silkily seductive voice. 'Believe when I say I'm *very* impressed with you.'

Their eyes clashed, and for the first time he didn't bother to hide the extent of his desire for her. It blazed, hot and strong, compelling her to keep staring deep into his eyes. Immediately that peculiar fear zoomed back into her face, but still she couldn't seem to drag her eyes away from his. Gradually, her fear changed to a flush of acute sexual awareness. Colour flooded her cheeks and her lips fell ever so slightly apart.

In that moment Luke knew that she would be his once again.

His sense of triumph was intense, and he might have kissed her then, if the lift doors hadn't opened to reveal another couple waiting to go down to dinner. Still feeling invincible, Luke put a masterful hand on her elbow and ushered her inside, thrilled to feel her arm quivering uncontrollably.

His thoughts were primitive and savage as they rode down to the first floor. He was secure in the knowledge that no matter what she said or did over dinner she would not refuse him afterwards.

Once out of the lift on the first floor, they soon found themselves alone again—Luke steering her right while the other couple turned left and headed for the La Mer restaurant, which was a more formal restaurant and not what Luke had wanted for this evening. A more relaxed atmosphere was preferable when seduction was on the menu for supper.

'You're hurting me,' she said shakily.

'Sorry,' he said, releasing his grip on her elbow to trail his fingers down her arm then link his hand with hers. 'I don't know my own strength sometimes. This better?'

He lifted their entwined hands and pressed the backs of her fingertips lightly to his lips. The heat which flooded her cheeks brought another wave of black triumph, as did the tremor which ricocheted through her. Luke felt it right down to her fingertips.

He held her flustered face for a long, long moment. 'We'd better go inside,' he said at last, with an intimate little smile, 'or they might think we're not turning up. Don't want them giving our table to someone else, do we? I don't know about you, but I'm suddenly awfully hungry...'

CHAPTER SEVEN

LUKE'S triumph was short-lived, as he should have expected. Rachel Manning was not the sort of female to relish being at a disadvantage for long—especially sexually.

Actually, he didn't begrudge her the sanctuary she found behind a rapid resumption of her usual composure. He rather admired the way she took hold of herself as he ushered her into the restaurant. The speed with which her heated cheeks cooled to a more dignified and very faint blush was testimony to a will of iron.

It gave Luke a glimpse of why he was so obsessed with this woman. She might be a lot of things, but never weak. Hell, no. She didn't know the meaning of the word.

'What a lovely view,' she said with superb style, after the waiter had departed with their drink order. 'We have the best table in the house.'

Which they did—right in the far corner, where the large plate glass windows met, providing them with a panoramic view on all sides. Although night had well and truly fallen, Terrigal was still a pretty sight, with the many streetlights showing the seaside town and the beach to advantage, their reflections sparkling like diamonds in the darkened water as it rolled in gentle waves onto the semicircle of golden sand.

Not that Luke was interested in views. His attention was all for the woman sitting opposite him.

Their eyes met momentarily, hers holding his quite coolly, revealing that she'd totally recovered from what had happened earlier.

Luke wasn't worried. He knew exactly what to do to whip her right back into that highly desirable state of flustered arousal. He would simply kiss her. No woman in all his wide range of experience had ever reacted to his kisses as she had done eighteen months before. He'd never forgotten those little whimpering noises, or the way she'd simply melted against him, like liquid velvet.

The waiter coming back with the bottle of white wine he'd ordered put a welcome halt to Luke's train of thought. He dragged his mind back from the minefield of his memories to sample the crisply cold Chablis, gave his nod of approval and relaxed in his chair while the waiter filled both their glasses, then wiggled the bottle into the portable ice-bucket.

'Time to tell me the story of your life, I think,' she said abruptly, once the waiter had departed.

'You'll be bored to tears.'

'Believe me, I won't.'

Luke frowned at the edge in her voice, then decided just to go along with what she wanted. Besides, if he told her about his own life then she might tell him about hers.

'I have no idea where to start,' he said.

'Then just answer my questions. How old are you?'

'Thirty-two.'

'Are your parents both living?'

'My mother is. Dad died a few years back, of a heart attack. Mum lives in Monterey, in the same house I was born in.'

'I'll bet you're an only child.'

'Not at all. I have two older brothers—both married and both breeding like rabbits. Well, not exactly. Andy has two children, Mark three.'

'And you've never been married?'

'No.'

'Are you living with anyone?'

'No.'

'Got a girlfriend?'

He looked her straight in the eye. 'No.'

She arched one eyebrow, then stopped her questions to take a sip of her wine, sighing as she replaced the glass onto the crisp white tablecloth. Her hand, he thought, was trembling a little, but her eyes were as cool as ever as they lifted to him, and a wry smile was playing on her lips. 'I'll bet you were very popular at school. And good at everything.'

'Yes and no. I *was* popular, but not at all good at everything. Sport, yes—I was crazy about soccer—but not schoolwork. I had a type of attention deficiency syndrome, where my mind would wander off in all directions—never on the subject I was supposed to be studying. My report cards all said the same. ''Would do better if only he would concentrate.'' Still, I knew I was going to become a professional photographer from the age of thirteen, so my poor grades didn't really matter.'

'What made you decide to become a photographer so young?'

'Dad gave me a camera for my twelfth birthday, and I was immediately hooked. I found I had a talent for taking really flattering shots of people. I also found I could make money out of that talent.'

He smiled at the memory. 'I took glam photos of the best looking girls in school, then beefcakey shots of the hunkiest guys, and made a fortune selling copies around the playground. I even put out a calendar each year, using the pick of the bunch. Got into a bit of trouble when the tax department showed up in my classroom one day and demanded to see my books.'

Luke laughed. 'Luckily, the money I'd made up till then was in a tin under my bed. They went away in the end, after I'd convinced them photography was just my hobby, and I used all the money I'd made to buy equipment.'

'Clever,' she murmured.

'Streetwise more than clever, Rachel. I'm no genius, but I've made a success of my life. So far,' he added a touch bitterly.

She frowned and stared down at the table. Luke found her silence irritating and swept up his wine glass. 'So, what shall we drink to?' he said. 'My success, or yours?'

She glanced up, her rueful little laugh startling him.

'Can I share the joke?'

'Not really. The joke's definitely on me—but it is funny, in a way.'

'Funny ha-ha, or funny peculiar?' he drawled, knowing full well why she found the situation ironic, but since he wasn't supposed to know he had to play dumb.

'I doubt either of those adjectives fit,' she said drily, and took a decent sip of wine. 'It's certainly not amusing, and "peculiar" seems such a pathetically inadequate word.'

'To describe what, Rachel?'

She lifted the glass towards him in a toast-like gesture. 'You... Me... Us...'

'But there is no us...yet.'

'No, but there will be, won't there? In a fashion, that is,' she added, dropping her eyes while she sipped her wine.

Luke straightened in the chair. 'Precisely what do you mean by...in a fashion...?'

Her shrug seemed superbly nonchalant, but he fancied that it hid a lot of tension.

'You know exactly what I mean, Luke. You intend seducing me later. But come tomorrow morning that will be it, won't it? Unless, of course, you're tempted to finish up early and have another romantic interlude during the afternoon. Either way, by the end of the day you'll get in your car, I'll get in mine, and we'll go our separate ways.'

Luke's fingers tightened around his wine glass. 'Is that so?' he said curtly, not bothering to deny a thing. It certainly fitted one of the possible scenarios he had fantasised as happening with her.

'Yes, that's so,' she said with a soft sigh.

Her air of weary resignation infuriated him. 'You sound like you have no say in the matter,' he bit out, angry with her for assuming he was that kind of man, and angry with her for admitting that she would give herself to him on a silver platter like that.

Her eyes moved slowly to his, and Luke flinched at the pain in their depths. 'I don't,' came her simple but strained admission.

Luke didn't know what to say. Or think. Something was going on here that he was not privy to. But once again the secrets were all on her side, and he was not going to be let in on them. He wondered if she was some kind of nymphomaniac who, once turned on, could not stop herself from surrendering to the object of her desire. Maybe her sexual needs were so strong on occasion that she became an almost unwilling victim of her own body.

It would explain how she had acted at the exhibition that night. Luke began to see her love life as a series of one-night stands with men who meant nothing to her but a means to an end.

'Care to explain that remark?' he said tautly.

'Does it require an explanation? Do you really care? Good God, you're going to get what you want, so why make a fuss? Look, I told you this morning that I needed you. You knew what I meant then, just as you know now. But if you insist on my spelling it out then I will.

'You're an extremely handsome, very sexy man, Luke, and I'm madly attracted to you. I haven't been with a man for quite some time, and I find myself wanting to make love to you so badly that to sit here and act normally is almost impossible.'

Luke blinked his shock at her, for her words did not match her manner, which remained so cool and controlled that he wondered if she was joking.

How long was 'quite some time'? he wondered dazedly. A fortnight? A month? Not eighteen months, that was for sure!

He felt his blood beginning to boil, and his temper along with it. 'Then why not just do it?' he snapped. 'Get up, take my hand and take me back to your room right now. Why torture yourself any longer? Don't be a coward, Rachel. *Do it*!'

She threw him a look which riveted him to his chair, stunning him with its fury and its passion. And then she laughed again—a mad, demonic chuckle which chilled his soul.

'You really know how to get under a woman's skin, don't you, Luke?' she muttered, draining the rest of her wine with one swallow. 'I'll bet you've had plenty of practice. But you're quite right,' she added, astonishing him by actually standing up and picking up her purse. 'This is all such hypocrisy. Let's go,' she said, and began to move off, her long legs carrying her quickly from the restaurant.

Luke caught up with her at the lifts, his face flaming from having to endure the embarrassment of inventing an excuse to the startled waiter, not to mention the many curious eyes which had stared at him as he'd raced after her.

'It's just as well no one knows me around here,' he flung at her.

'Or me,' she retorted, her cheeks pinkening as well. 'You think I'd be doing this if anyone around here knew me?'

'Frankly, I don't know what to think,' he bit out truthfully.

'Then don't,' she snapped. 'Just do what you usually do. Take what's on offer, and don't ask any questions.'

He glared at her through narrowed eyes, fearing at that moment what he might do to her. Maybe she saw the troubled turbulence in his gaze, or maybe she had a sudden crisis of conscience. All he knew was that her face unexpectedly began to crumple, her hands flying up to try to hide her distress.

'Oh, God,' she cried. 'God...'

There were no actual tears, just a moaning sound which tore into Luke's guts. Her shoulders began to shake while she struggled for control. Unable to help himself, he gathered her into a comforting embrace, holding her tight against him as they waited for a lift.

'I'm sorry,' she choked out between shudders. 'So sorry...'

'Hush,' he soothed. 'Hush.'

'S-sorry,' she repeated raggedly.

'Me too,' he rasped, moved beyond words as she continued to tremble violently against him.

The lift doors opened and it was blessedly empty. Luke bundled her in, one arm staying wrapped around her while he punched the floor number.

'Here, give me this,' he said, removing the purse which was clenched defensively between them and was digging into Luke's ribs. He tucked it under his left arm then reached up to stroke her head, smoothing down the glossy blonde hair and pressing her face against his chest. She turned her head with a shuddering sigh to lay her cheek against him, the trusting gesture sending a sweet, curling sensation all through him.

Her rag-doll limpness evoked the same possessive protectiveness and tenderness in him which he'd felt for her during their first encounter. Where before it had thrown him, Luke now accepted it as perfectly reasonable. How else was he supposed to feel about the woman he loved?

He almost laughed at his own stupidity in having denied it for so long, at having listened to his own desperate reasonings.

You don't know anything about her, he'd tried telling himself many times over. You only spent one short evening with her. Love at first sight is just so much romantic rubbish. She's a slut, a whore, a...a...rotten damned adulteress! You can't possibly be in love with her!

But he was.

It wasn't logical, or reasonable, or even sensible. Clearly, she was one highly mixed-up woman. But, despite all that, he still loved her.

'Rachel,' he whispered, wanting to hear her name on his lips.

She lifted her strained face and he bent to press light lips on her forehead, then on her nose, followed by each cheek, and ending up at her softly parted lips. Her sharply sucked-in breath told him all he needed to know at that moment.

He kissed her, and it was exactly as he remembered. The sensuality of her mouth. The little sounds she made deep in her throat. The total surrendering of her body to his. She was clinging to him when the lift doors opened, and it took a moment for either of them to realise that there were people waiting to get in.

Luke summoned up a suave smile from somewhere, and swept a limp Rachel past the staring couple. She'd managed to find her feet a little better by the time they made it to her room, but remained shaken and silent while he opened the door with the key in her purse and ushered her inside. She stared at him while he tossed the key and the purse onto the bedside table then began taking off his jacket.

He smiled reassuringly at her, rather liking her silence and her hesitation. He draped his jacket over a nearby chair and began to attack his shirt.

'Luke,' she suddenly burst out.

His hand froze on the second button of his shirt, instinct warning him that he was not going to like what she was about to say.

'What?' came his curt query.

'I...I...I hope you've got some protection with you...'

His relief was mixed with some irony. So she wanted him to use something tonight, did she? No more mad risks? No more being totally carried away?

'That goes without saying,' he said brusquely. 'I'm not in the habit of taking insane chances.'

She blushed fiercely, her eyes unhappy as they dropped to the floor. Luke could see that things were in danger of deteriorating, so he did what any sensible desire-ravaged man would have done. He stopped undressing and stalked over to drag her into his arms again, his mouth descending with a hunger and force which brooked no more nonsense or delay.

It came as little surprise that she seemed to relish his mad display of passion, moaning beneath the savage sweeps of his tongue then actually matching his passion by wrapping her arms tightly around his waist.

He responded by sliding his own hands down over her buttocks and pulling her hard against him, all his stomach muscles contracting at the feel of his erection pressed into the mound above her sex. He only just managed to keep a lid on his wildly flaring arousal.

Till she made a rotating movement with her hips.

'God, Rachel,' he gasped as he burst away from her, raking both his hands through his hair while he battled to control his throbbing flesh. 'You shouldn't do things like that. Not at this point.'

'I suppose not,' she agreed huskily. 'But you do have an unfortunate effect on me.'

'Unfortunate?' he repeated, his nostrils flaring when her hands lifted to the top button of her jacket. 'How do you mean . . . unfortunate?'

A strange smile played on her lips while her hands moved tantalisingly down her front, undoing each button as she went. 'You make me do things I know I shouldn't. You make me . . . weak . . . and wicked,' she added, parting her jacket and pushing it back off her shoulders.

Luke's breath caught in his throat. For she was naked underneath, had been all along.

The silky top slid down her arms and fluttered away onto the carpet. Luke sucked in another sharp breath when her hands went to her waist and she began to slip the silk trousers down over her hips, taking her underwear with her.

She had to bend over to complete the action, and those glorious hard-tipped breasts swung away from her body, twin orbs of lush perfection. Various erotic tableaux teased his brain, sending torturous messages from his brain to his body. His loins filled with a dull, heavy ache the like of which he'd never known before.

He had to have her, and he had to have her quickly.

'For pity's sake, Rachel,' he practically implored when she straightened, even the simple action of her tossing her hair back from her shoulders bringing a flash of unbearable discomfort.

There was no pity for him, however, in her glazed green eyes. 'Now you,' she ordered huskily.

'Me?'

'Yes. I want to undress you.'

His groan finally communicated his hell to her.

But, if her smile was anything to go by, the knowledge evoked a perverse pleasure in her, not pity. 'Poor Luke,' she murmured, stepping forward to reach up on tiptoe and kiss him lightly on the lips, her naked nipples brushing his chest. 'I won't take too long,' she said huskily, busy fingers nimbly flicking open the remaining buttons on his shirt.

But then she slowed, taking her time in peeling the shirt back from his tensely squared shoulders and feasting her eyes over his bared chest.

'God, but you're beautiful,' she said thickly, and spread both her hands over the curls in the centre of his chest. 'Beautiful,' she repeated, and began rubbing her satin-soft palms out over the broad flat muscles which housed his male nipples, trailing repeatedly over them till they tightened into round hard pebbles of heightened sensitivity.

'Don't blame me if this doesn't work out as well as you hope,' he warned darkly, struggling desperately for control as she went about her ruthless journey of discovery.

She didn't answer. She merely smiled and bent to lick where her fingers had been.

Luke bit his bottom lip and let her do it for a while, loving yet hating the way his stomach somersaulted at every sweep of her tongue. But when she actually took one of the taut nubs between her teeth, and tugged it none too gently, he grabbed her shoulders and wrenched her head away.

'That's enough of that,' he growled, putting her from him quite firmly then stripping off the rest of his clothes himself. While he was at it he rummaged through his pockets to find his wallet, extracting some protection before he was beyond caring.

He could not believe it when she took the condom from his wildly unsteady hands, knelt down and did the job for him. Her expertise shattered any secret hope he might have harboured about how often she'd done this type of thing. Hell, her idea of not having had a man for a long time was probably three whole days!

God, if only she'd take her hands off him. If only she'd stop caressing him. He couldn't take much more of such intimate foreplay. Not this first time.

No, don't do that, for pity's sake, he screamed silently, even as he let her. Oh, sweet Jesus...

'Rachel,' he choked out at last. 'You simply must stop.'

She ignored him.

'Didn't you hear what I said?' he groaned, dragging her upright and shaking her.

Her bewildered blinking told him how far she'd retreated from reality. She was breathing heavily, but then so was he. Luke stared at her mouth, that pouting, panting mouth, which only moments before had brought him right to the edge.

He was still on the edge, damn it.

'Make love to me, Luke,' she had the hide to say at that point, and she sidled against him once more.

Luke's blood pressure reached new heights, as did his frustration. 'You haven't given me much of a chance.'

'I know,' she rasped, lifting her right leg and sliding her thigh provocatively up and down the outside of his. 'I wanted to be ready for you. I'm ready now, Luke. Do it to me now.'

He needed little encouragement, and surged inside her, groaning with pleasure and dismay when he felt himself begin to come almost immediately. Hell, he knew he wasn't going to be able to hang on. She was so hot and wet and wild, writhing and rotating on him till nothing was going to stop his desire exploding. He gritted his teeth and tried to will it away, but nothing could stop him. Nothing.

He cried out his agony and ecstasy, holding her tightly as he shuddered violently into her. Just as his male ego began to tip him into despair she did the most incredible thing. She came too, her flesh answering his in the most intensely mutual release he had ever experienced. Their bodies throbbed as one, pulsing deep within each other, bringing a physical and emotional satisfaction to Luke which quite blew him away.

They fell onto the bed together, their bodies still fused, both still climaxing uncontrollably. Luke rolled her on top of him, where he grasped her buttocks and kept rocking her against him, seeking to prolong the sensations, not wanting them ever to end. Finally they both became still, with Rachel

collapsed across him. She moaned one last moan
against his chest, her arms flopping wide on the
bed in an attitude of total exhaustion and satiation.

Luke felt as if he'd just run a marathon, his heart
still pounding. All that could be heard in the room
was his ragged breathing. But gradually his blood
calmed down, and the room became very quiet. He
was beginning to think he just might live to make
love again in the near future when a jarring sound
broke the silence.

Wide green eyes jolted immediately open, to stare
at the telephone by the bed. Luke scowled his impatience at the interruption, then frowned at
Rachel's obvious alarm.

Who on earth, he wondered, was ringing her
room at this hour? And why did she look so
damned worried all of a sudden?

CHAPTER EIGHT

'AREN'T you going to answer it?' Luke said after a few more rings. 'This is your room, after all.'

'Well...er...um...' She glanced down at where their bodies were still intimately joined.

Luke came pretty close to blushing. 'Right,' he muttered, easing away from her and swinging his legs over the side of the bed, thankfully on the opposite side of the bed to the telephone. 'You can answer it now,' he added as he stood up and stalked off towards the bathroom.

He shouldn't have done it, he supposed. Hurried to do what he had to do, then sneakily opened the bathroom door just far enough so that he could listen to what she was saying.

But he had, telling himself that he simply had to find out all he could about the woman he loved—especially since she wasn't about to offer any information. He needed knowledge if he was to get past this hard protective shell she'd built around herself.

'So what did the doctor think?' she was saying, when he first tuned in to her side of the conversation. 'Are you sure, Sarah? I could quite easily come home for tonight and drive back in the morning. I'm sure I can talk the photographer into letting me start a bit later or delaying the shoot another day. If not, he'll just have to find himself another model. The money's not that important, compared to my son's health.'

Luke gripped the doorknob. A *son*? She already had a son!

Black jealousy speared through him, mixed with torment over her dismissive attitude towards him. And there he'd been thinking he must mean something special to her for her body to respond to him so swiftly and totally.

The realisation that he'd just been callously used once again filled him with dismay and disgust. It added to her guilt, somehow, that she'd only cheated on her husband eighteen months before, but had done so after having had his baby. God, but she was despicable!

'No, Sarah, I've made up my mind,' she swept on firmly. 'I'm coming home right away. I know there's nothing much I can do but sit with him, but I won't be able to sleep tonight anyway for worrying. If I leave straight away I should be there in well under two hours. The traffic will be light at this hour. See you then, Sarah... Yes, I will... Bye.'

She hung up and turned, still nude, to find him standing at the foot of the bed, equally buck naked, glaring his frustration at her. 'Yes, I will, what?' he demanded sharply.

'Yes, I...I will drive carefully,' she returned, her momentary stammer the only evidence that the situation was in any way rattling her. 'That was my mother-in-law,' she explained hurriedly. 'I told you she'd been sick. Well, she's taken a turn for the worse. I have to go home. I can drive back up here tomorrow, if you insist.'

'Don't bother lying to me, Rachel,' he snapped. 'I heard everything.'

He rather enjoyed seeing her go pale. He would enjoy seeing the bitch go a damned sight paler before he let her go this time.

'You never mentioned that you had a child,' he added coldly.

Now heat raced back into her pale cheeks. 'You were listening!' she accused him, and he almost laughed at her indignation. The pot was calling the kettle black!

'It seemed the only way to find out anything about you,' he said testily. 'You do have this passion for secrecy. And secrets. So, I ask you again, why didn't you tell me you had a son?' Even as he said the words, the most ghastly suspicion began to form in the back of his mind.

'Why should I?' she tossed back, momentarily throwing him with her offhand manner. 'My son is none of your business. If you must know, having a baby is not always good for business. Now, if you'll excuse me,' she said, scooping up her scattered clothes from the floor, 'I have to get dressed and get going.'

'And you have to come back tomorrow and finish this job,' he demanded, all the while desperately trying to push that irrational suspicion to the back of his mind. For it just couldn't be true. It was too fanciful for words. Even *she* wouldn't be *that* wicked.

But, damn it all, he didn't like the word 'baby'. Initially he'd imagined her child to be a small boy, of maybe two or three. A baby suggested less than a year old. Dear God, what if he was only nine months old? What if...?

'I don't *have* to do anything,' she threw at him as she straightened, clutching the clothes in front of her nakedness. 'I quit. Find yourself another blonde. I'm sure you won't have any trouble. You know what they say, Luke. Variety is the spice of life.'

His hands balled into fists by his sides, and for a few seconds Luke warred with a thousand primitive emotions—not the least of which was the desire for murder.

He watched, seething, as she turned her back on him and disappeared into the bathroom.

By the time she came out of the bathroom a couple of minutes later, fully dressed, he too had dragged on his clothes and was sitting on the side of the bed. He watched while she packed the rest of her things, torn between wanting to ask her the critical question and remaining silent.

Better you don't know, came the voice of common sense. Let her go, man. She's bad news.

But ignorance was not bliss in the end. He could not bear not to know.

'How old is your son, Rachel?' he asked abruptly.

Her shock at his question was so acute that Luke was almost sick on the spot. Dear God, no, he groaned to himself.

'Why...why do you want to know?' she asked shakily, her face as white as a sheet.

Luke jumped to his feet and swore. Then swore again. Violently. Obscenely. He wanted to weep, but it just wasn't the done thing. Men didn't blubber. They swore. So he swore a third time and glared his hatred at her. Hatred would sustain him, he hoped.

She stared back at him with eyes like saucers, her mouth gaping. He saw her shock change to outrage, her lips snapping shut and her eyes flashing fury at him. 'You bastard,' she hissed. 'You knew who I was all along!'

His top lip curled with contempt at her indignation. 'Yes, of course. That's why I hired you. I knew I was on to a sure thing. Now, answer my question, damn you! How old is your son? And don't bother to lie. I can find out easily enough now that I know of his existence.'

'Eleven months,' she snapped, her own attitude just as contemptuous of him. 'Too old to be yours, lover. So you don't have to worry. You can continue on your merry way without the millstone of an unwanted child around your oh, so handsome neck! My baby is my husband's child. Patrick Reginald Cleary, the third.'

Luke wasn't sure if he was relieved or revolted. So she'd already been a couple of months pregnant that night—a son and heir already growing inside her. If it *was* her husband's child, that was!

Still, it explained why she hadn't been worried about not using protection. Being pregnant had freed her to fulfil all her sexual fantasies without being caught out.

'You rotten bitch,' he said in a low quaking voice. 'You filthy rotten bitch. Get out of here before I kill you.'

Her stricken look produced no pity in him. He could find no excuse for her behaviour in his heart. On top of that, he could find no excuse for himself, for feeling perversely disappointed that the child wasn't his. This was not a woman worth loving! She wasn't worth spitting on!

'Get out!' he snarled through gritted teeth.

She gave him one last anguished look, grabbed her things and fled, leaving the door open behind her. Luke stormed over and slammed it, then paced furiously about the room, raking his hands repeatedly through his hair.

'I do not believe this,' he muttered to himself. 'None of it makes sense. It doesn't feel right.'

Luke ground to an abrupt halt, black eyes flinging wide.

That's because it *isn't* right, man, came the astoundingly certain answer.

Luke gasped, then grimaced. Oh, my God, what if she'd lied about the baby's age? What if he wasn't eleven months old? What if she'd called his bluff about finding out the child's age and simply added two months? Clearly she hadn't thought he was all that interested in the baby as such, anyway. She saw him as the swinging bachelor-type of photographer—going from woman to woman, model to model, one-night stand to one-night stand.

Luke's insides began to churn, his gut feeling telling him that he'd just come to the right conclusion. The child *was* his! It was the only logical answer to her reactions to him—the only thing that made any sense at all. My God, it explained so much. About tonight and about eighteen months ago.

'I have no time for cowards tonight,' was what she'd said back then.

Which had been oh, so true, he thought bitterly. She'd wanted a child and her husband had obviously not been able to give her one—her much older and possibly ill husband. So she'd gone out and got herself one, the same way women had been getting themselves babies and heirs since time immemorial—by seducing some poor unsuspecting devil—namely himself!

But she'd run into snags with him from the first, hadn't she? To begin with he'd surprised her, by taking over the lovemaking and insisting on using protection. That had been why she'd had to seduce him a second time. *Really* seduce him, so that he'd been so turned on he was beyond caring about the risk. After which she'd coolly done a flit without leaving a clue as to her identity.

Of course, she had to have planned all that in advance—booking the hotel room in a false name, paying by cash and not credit card. Every single move had been planned—from her provocative clothing right down to her selection of a suitable candidate.

Luke wondered sourly what it had been about him which had made her choose him. His looks, perhaps, or just his having been alone? Had it merely been chance which had drawn him into her web of deceit, or had there been a perverse destiny behind it all?

She'd never expected to run into him again. Hell, why should she have? She'd thought he was an American tourist. But when their paths had crossed again, and she'd been given the let-off by his seemingly not recognising her, she'd run into a second snag.

She'd found that she actually still fancied him, sexually speaking.

Luke had been with enough woman to know that she'd really fancied him the first time too. More, perhaps, than she'd ever anticipated—so much so that she simply could not resist having another sampling of his services.

Which brought him full circle to what he'd thought about her in the first place. She was a rotten bitch—a cold, calculating slut who at this very moment was on her way out of his life a second time. Only this time she was taking his son with her!

Over my dead body, he vowed darkly.

Luke acted quickly and decisively, racing down to his room, collecting his car keys and setting off after her. He figured that he'd easily catch up with her on the expressway to Sydney. That small Nissan of hers couldn't do what his Ford could do, and she'd be easy enough to spot at this hour of the night, with few cars on the road. The dark would also mean he'd be able to follow her without being observed in her rear-vision mirror.

He spotted her car shortly after Mount White, keeping well back till the expressway ended, after which he had to move closer or risk being left behind at red lights. As it was, he did lose her at one intersection for a few minutes, but luckily he knew the roads south of the city quite well, and knew where he would catch up.

The digital clock on the dashboard showed just on eleven when she finally turned from the main road, not far from the Cronulla shopping centre. Luke dropped back a bit as he too turned left, pulling over to the kerb and switching off his headlights when he saw her brakelights come on and stay on. He watched as she turned into a driveway a hundred metres or so up the street, the car disappearing down the far side of a house.

When he was sure that she'd had enough time to go inside, he climbed out of the car and walked along to stand and stare at the house which he believed held his son.

It was an old brick-veneer cottage, with a red-tiled roof, a ramshackle carport attached and lawns which needed mowing.

Luke frowned. If this was where Rachel was living, then she *hadn't* come out of her marriage flushed with money. His assumption that she'd wanted to provide an heir for the Cleary family fortune had clearly been amiss. Unless unforeseen circumstance had somehow dissipated any wealth. People *had* been known to make bad investments—to lose all their money in one fell swoop.

Luke gave himself a mental shake. There was no use trying to second-guess Rachel or her motivations. No use confronting her either. She would simply lie to him again. He would have to be far more devious than that in finding out the truth of the matter.

Luke noted the number on the postbox, then walked up to the nearest corner, where he memorised the street name. On his way back down past the house he stopped for a few moments to stare some more.

What if you're wrong, Luke? a niggling voice whispered. What if he's not your son? What if...?

'I'm not wrong,' he growled aloud. 'I just know it!' And, whirling on his heels, he strode back down the street towards his car.

CHAPTER NINE

LUKE didn't drive back up to Terrigal. He went home, from where he rang the hotel, told them there had been a family emergency back in Sydney and asked them to pack his things in his bag—which was in the bottom of the wardrobe in his room—and send it down by courier. He also asked them to check Miss Manning's room, in case she'd left anything behind, and do likewise. They were to bill everything to his credit card, of which they already had an imprint.

He had just hung up the telephone in the front hallway when his mother emerged from her bedroom, looking bleary-eyed and bewildered.

'I thought I heard your voice, Luke. What are you doing home? I thought you said you were staying up on the coast tonight.'

'I was. But things didn't quite work out as I'd hoped.'

Grace couldn't say that she was sorry. Luke had given her some story about doing some photographs for Theo around the Central Coast beaches, but she'd suspected all along that he'd gone away with a woman—probably that married one he was mixed up with.

Frankly, Grace was both surprised and disappointed in Luke for having anything to do with a married woman in the first place. It wasn't like him at all. For all his being a nineties man in a lot of ways, he'd always held fairly old-fashioned views in matters of morals and marriage.

Unless, of course, he hadn't known she was married till after he'd become emotionally and physically involved. Now, that was a likely explanation...

Dear me, but the poor love looked all done-in, and quite shattered. Still, it was all for the best if he'd broken up with *that* type.

'Want a cup of tea, love?' she asked gently.

'That'd be great, Mum.'

Grace smiled ruefully as she made her way out to the kitchen. At least she was still good for something, if only making cups of tea.

'And a toasted sandwich wouldn't go astray, either,' Luke added as he followed her. 'I...er...didn't get round to having any dinner.'

Grace glanced over her shoulder at him, her mouth opening to ask him why on earth not, but another look at Luke's bleak face closed it again. Not tonight, she decided wisely. He wasn't in a fit state for the third degree tonight. Maybe tomorrow.

'In that case sit down and I'll get you one,' she said briskly, and began filling the electric jug.

She heard him scrape out a kitchen chair behind her and slump down into it. 'Thanks, Mum,' he said, a grim weariness in his actions and his words.

Grace resolved not to ask him about his miserable mood, or the reason behind it. Luke would be returning to America in ten days or so, which would no doubt be the end of the affair for once and for all. At least, she hoped so...

Luke woke to depression and indecisiveness, but he ruthlessly pushed both aside. There was nothing to be gained by wallowing in self-pity and doubt. Nothing to be gained by wondering and worrying. Hamlet had waffled for too long, and look where that had got him.

Luke's job this morning was to glean the truth, after which his course of action would become clear. One step at a time, he vowed. Find out if the boy is yours first.

Strange, but he didn't feel quite as sure of that this morning as he had last night.

Luke lay in bed for ages, tracing over everything Rachel had ever said and done, including that mini-breakdown in front of the lifts. What had her repeated apologies meant? What had she been saying sorry for? Surely not just her behaviour in the restaurant? True, she'd acted pretty badly, but was it more logical that she had been saying sorry for having used him to father a child, without his knowledge or consent?

Damn, but it was all so confusing and confounding!

Luke threw back the bedclothes and bounced out of bed before he went bonkers. Time to find out for sure, Luke. Time to get some answers.

*   *   *

He sat low behind the wheel of his mother's battered old blue sedan, biting his fingernails while he watched and waited for his opportunity.

Not a soul had stirred all morning, and it was nearly eleven. He'd hoped to catch a glimpse of the child, perhaps—though on reflection a baby under one year old wouldn't play in the yard. He probably couldn't even walk yet! His life would largely be indoors, unless either Rachel or the mother-in-law took him out in a pram or a stroller or whatever.

Another half-hour passed, and Luke was about to make the decision to go up to the front door and just knock when that same front door opened and Rachel emerged, wearing jeans and a long-sleeved blue top. She turned to speak to a white-haired lady in the doorway, her own long blonde hair caught up in a ponytail. Suddenly she whirled and hurried down the front steps with what looked like a purse in her right hand.

Luke slid further down in the seat till he could only just see her, but, as he'd hoped, she didn't give the old blue car across the road a second glance as she walked quickly down the front path and through the slightly rickety front gate.

Luke came back upright once she'd taken off up the street, letting out a shuddering sigh when she turned right at the corner and headed in the direction of the shopping centre, which he knew was a good ten-minute walk away. Even if she was able to buy whatever she wanted in five minutes flat, he still had a conservative twenty-five-minute leeway to find out all he needed to know.

His heart thudding heavily behind his ribs, he climbed out of the car, thankful that he'd taken the trouble to dress well. He didn't want the old lady being suspicious of him in any way. He had to charm his way right into that house and into her confidence in five minutes flat.

Luke's first shock came when Rachel's mother-in-law answered the door. For, although she did have white hair, she was not even remotely an *old* lady. She looked no older than his own mother, who was in her mid-sixties. How old, then, had Patrick Cleary been? Maybe not as old as Luke had assumed.

'Mrs Cleary?' Luke asked, smoothing any shock from his face and finding his most winning smile.

'Yes,' the lady returned hesitantly.

'Goodness, you look too young to be Rachel's mum-in-law,' he said, actually meaning the words even as he recognised the remark as an obviously flattering line which men used on women all the time.

He felt quite guilty when it worked, her pale cheeks pinkening with pleasure.

'I'm Luke St Clair, Mrs Cleary,' he went on while she was still slightly flushed and flustered. 'I'm the photographer Rachel was working with yesterday. Is she home? I need to talk to her about rescheduling the rest of the shoot. I really don't want to use another model. As I'm sure you understand, not too many models have that special quality and style which Rachel has.'

'Oh, dear, you just missed her. But she won't be long. She's just popped down to the chemist to pick up some more medicine for Derek's gums. The poor baby's having teething troubles—but I suppose she told you that.'

'Derek?' Luke repeated, taken aback a second time. 'I thought her son was called Patrick?'

'Really? How odd. Maybe you misunderstood. Patrick was his father's name. Actually, his father *did* want him to be called Patrick, after himself and his grandfather, but Rachel—sensible girl that she is—put her foot down and said that that type of thing went out with the Dark Ages. I have to admit I agree with her. I didn't want to call my Patrick Patrick when he was born, but my husband insisted, and women in those days went along with what their husbands wanted more than they do nowadays.'

She gave a wan little smile, which Luke wasn't sure how to interpret, although he'd somehow gained the impression that Mrs Cleary's relationship with her husband had not been all she'd wanted it to be. Still, he could see that she was a softie—one of those refined, delicate old-world women, who didn't have the spirit or the strength to stand up for themselves. Confrontation was not their style at all.

'Goodness, how I am rattling on,' she dithered. 'And you still out on the doorstep, Mr St Clair. You must think me very rude. Do come in.'

'Call me Luke,' he insisted as he followed her down a neat narrow hallway then into an equally neat but cluttered lounge-room. There was much too much furniture and knick-knacks for the size of the room, and, although some were pieces of obvious quality, a lot of them were worn and just a little shabby.

'Then you must call me Sarah,' the old lady tittered back, and Luke's conscience pricked again. It didn't feel right, worming his way into this sweet old darling's confidence. But it had to be done!

'I'll just pop out to the kitchen and make some tea,' she said. 'Do make yourself at home.'

Luke let out a long-held breath once he was alone. He hadn't realised till that moment just how tense he was.

Some wedding photographs on the wall immediately drew Luke's attention, and he slowly picked his way between the furniture to get closer, his frown deepening as it became clear that the man standing beside Rachel was far from elderly. Grey hair he might have had back then, but it must have been premature, for the handsome smiling face beaming out at Luke from inside that silver frame belonged to a man no older than his mid-thirties— if that!

It rather blasted away one of his preconceptions about Rachel, as had this house last night. She had not married some old man for money, which meant that she must have married for love.

Luke tore his tortured gaze away from the wedding pictures, his eyes narrowing and swinging around the room in search of what he knew had to be there somewhere.

And then he saw it—a baby photograph, sitting on top of a beautifully carved bookcase which was half hidden behind a couple of overstuffed chintzy armchairs.

He swallowed, and squeezed between the arms to pick up the silver-framed picture. The baby in the ten-by-eight coloured print looked about six months old, and was stark naked, sitting in a bath. He was an extremely beautiful child, with soft blond curls covering his head and the brightest blue eyes Luke had ever seen.

Luke's chest tightened. His own eyes were such a dark brown people thought them black. Dark brown eyes were dominant in his family, on both sides. Even though Rachel had green eyes, Luke himself would have had to carry a recessive blue gene to have a blue-eyed child.

He didn't think that he carried that gene. His two brothers definitely didn't, all their five children having brown eyes. It had often been a matter of family discussion, their dark brown eyes.

A sudden thought struck Luke, and he hurried back to peer at the wedding photos. Damn it all but it looked as if Rachel's husband had had brown eyes as well. Not as dark brown as his, however.

One of Luke's other suspicions about Rachel returned with a vengeance. The baby might not be his, but he might not be her husband's either. It would explain why she'd been so adamant about not calling the baby Patrick. Doing so would have been a constant reminder of her guilt.

Luke decided not to waste any further time. He would find out the child's exact age, then get the hell out of here. Taking the baby's photograph with him as a talking point, he easily found the kitchen in the small house, where Sarah Cleary was busy making up a teatray.

She looked up with a ready smile, making Luke feel rotten again. 'Oh, so you've found Derek's picture. Such a beautiful child, don't you think? There again, he has an exceptionally beautiful mother.'

Luke found a dark irony in the woman's generosity in giving most of the credit for the child's looks to the mother. Little did she know that it was possible her own son had contributed a big zero to the boy's beauty. No doubt there was some handsome blue-eyed hunk somewhere around Australia—or maybe the world—who was equally ignorant of the contribution he'd made to the Cleary family.

'Rachel said he turns one next month,' Luke said innocently, and held his breath for the answer.

'Yes, that's right,' Sarah tripped back, and Luke's heart hit rock bottom. 'October the fourteenth.'

Self-disgust was hard on the heels of his disappointment.

Good God, don't tell me I was still hoping, despite the blue eyes. What kind of fool am I?

The kind who just doesn't know when to quit, came back the rueful answer.

He was searching his mind for some excuse to go and have a look at the child, whom he assumed must be asleep, when the house was rent by the sound of a child's cries. They were high-pitched and quite loud, more like a temper tantrum than the sounds of a distressed baby.

His eyes flew to Sarah, who didn't look all that concerned. 'It seems Master Derek has awakened from his morning nap. I know he sounds like he's distressed, but he's not. He's just bored. He can't bear being in bed once he's awake. Would you mind pouring yourself some tea while I get him up, Luke?'

'Er... not at all.' Luke glanced at his watch and saw that only fifteen minutes had gone by since he had entered the house. With a bit of luck he would still be away before Madame Lash returned from the shops.

'I'll be a minute or two,' Sarah warned him. 'I'll have to change his nappy before he makes an appearance in public.'

The crocodile tears were becoming louder and more demanding. What a little tyrant, Luke thought, yet found himself smiling when the sounds stopped abruptly the moment Sarah opened his bedroom door.

Luke poured himself a cup of tea and was sitting, dunking in a biscuit, when Sarah came back, carrying a dry-eyed Derek who looked considerably older and even more good-looking than in his photograph. Never had Luke seen such beautiful big brown...

'Brown,' he choked out, after almost choking on the biscuit.

'What's that, dear?' Sarah said as she slid the baby boy into the highchair at the end of the table. The job completed, child and grandmother both turned curious looks on him.

'His eyes,' Luke repeated dazedly. 'They're brown. But they're blue here in this photograph.' He picked up the frame to stare at those bright blue eyes once more.

Sarah's laugh was soft and gentle. 'Didn't you know? All babies are born with blue eyes. Some take several months before they change to their final colour. Derek's eyes are exactly the same colour as his father's eyes. Really, it's the only part of his father that he's inherited.'

Luke felt that sick feeling once more. She was right. Derek's eyes were not nearly as dark as his own—more like the mid-brown of Patrick Cleary's.

His sigh carried a resigned finality. He'd come full circle, hadn't he? With all his preconceptions about Derek's conception now well and truly routed. Rachel had been guilty of one night of infidelity, that was all. One mad night when, for whatever reasons best known to herself, she'd simply needed a man.

And she'd chosen him.

Dear God, why me? he groaned silently.

He now wished he had not come—wished that he'd listened to that other voice which had told him to leave well enough alone.

But he *had* come, and would have to stay and face Rachel, who would no doubt be furious with him. Ahh, well...

'Is he a difficult baby?' Luke asked, more to make conversation than out of any real interest. The child was not his. His instinct had failed him for the first time in his life.

Sarah handed the baby a fruit stick to chew on and sat down to pour herself some tea.

'He's been a right pain,' Sarah admitted. 'But he's getting better. Of course, Rachel fusses over him far too much—but that's understandable, considering his precarious start to life.'

'Oh? He was a sickly baby, was he?'

'Well, not exactly. Just premature. Two whole months. He spent the first six weeks of his life in a humidicrib.'

Luke was glad that Sarah chose that moment to stand up and tie a bib around the baby's neck, for Luke knew that his face must have shown his feelings. There was no rage. Just shock, followed by a wave of intense elation which threatened to undermine every ounce of control he was desperately trying to muster. Dear God, he almost burst into tears!

Luke's eyes still watered as they turned to stare at his son. It was totally involuntary, the love that welled up in his heart for the boy, the all-consuming feeling of pride and paternal joy. His eyes locked with the child's, and maybe he communicated his emotion to his offspring, for the child seemed transfixed with his father, his big brown eyes rounding further.

'Derek,' he said softly, and a happy gurgle erupted from those baby lips, his arms flapping in a gesture of uninhibited delight.

Sarah smiled at her guest as she sat back down. 'He likes you, Luke. Which is a first. He doesn't usually like men. Of course,' she added with a sad little sigh, 'he hasn't had much contact with them. I suppose Rachel told you Derek's father died when he was only a couple of weeks old?'

'Er... actually no, she didn't. But I knew she was a widow when I hired her. What did your son die from, Sarah?'

'Leukaemia. He was diagnosed about a year after he and Rachel were married. After some intensive chemotherapy he went into remission for a year or so, but then it flared up again, worse than ever, and we all knew it was only a matter of time. Patrick only lasted as long as he did because Rachel was expecting his baby. He'd always wanted a son, you see. Quite obsessively. I can't tell you how relieved I was when Rachel's ultrasound showed she was having a boy.'

'It must have been a difficult time for all of you,' he murmured.

'It was, but Rachel was marvellous. That girl has such strength, you've no idea. I would have fallen apart if it hadn't been for her. She means the world to me—as, of course, does little Derek here. We've both got him to thank for pulling us through the bad spots. Being responsible for another human being does make you snap out of self-pity, and it gives you a purpose in life.'

Luke was trying to find some answer to that when the front door banged, and three seconds later Rachel swept into the kitchen, speaking as she went.

'I bought some gel for Derek's gums and some infant dose Pana—' Her voice broke off when she spotted Luke sitting there, all the blood draining from her face.

CHAPTER TEN

ODDLY enough, Luke's reaction to her distress was not anger or resentment, but pity. No sensible-thinking man could have looked upon that lovely pale face with its haunted green eyes and imagined for one moment that she was wicked or, God forbid, some kind of conscienceless whore. Whatever had driven her to do what she had done eighteen months ago, it had not been selfish desire or nymphomaniacal need.

It had been desperation.

Of that he was certain. Desperation to give her dying husband the son he'd always wanted.

'Luke,' was all she could manage to say, the word as strained as her expression.

'Hello, Rachel,' he returned, trying to put her at ease. 'I dropped by to see when you might be free to finish the shoot. Sarah here said you wouldn't be long, then kindly invited me in for tea.'

'Yes, and you should see how Derek has taken to him, Rachel,' Sarah chimed on, oblivious to the underlying tension in the room. 'Why, he was laughing and smiling a moment ago. I was telling Luke, that's not like him at all. Most men make him go all quiet and shy. See—he's smiling at Luke right now.'

'Yes, yes, I see,' Rachel said stiffly, although some colour had come back into her face. Obviously she'd begun clinging to the hope that nothing had been said or done to give the game away.

Luke decided that he wasn't going to allow her to play that game any more. But he was not so cruel or insensitive as to say anything in front of Sarah.

'Rachel, I really do need to have a private word with you,' Luke said firmly, which brought another panic-stricken glance from those dark-ringed green eyes. She really did look awfully tired this morning, but still incredibly beautiful.

'Why don't you take Luke into the lounge-room, Rachel?' Sarah offered. 'I'll take Derek out into the yard for a play in his sandpit. And don't worry. I'll put some sunscreen and a hat on him.' This with a rueful smile at Luke, as if to say, See what I mean? Such a fusspot of a mother!

'All right,' Rachel said, lifting her son out of the highchair, her face going all soft and glowing as she gave him a peck on the cheek. 'You be a good boy for your nan—and no tantrums, mind. When she says it's time to come inside then it's time to come in. Only fifteen minutes at this time of day, Sarah. Luke and I should be finished by then.'

Luke returned her challenging glance with a bland face, not wanting to tip his hand in advance.

'This way,' she said coolly once Sarah and Derek had departed for the great outdoors. 'First door on the left.'

Luke felt his chest tightening as she waved him ahead of her out of the kitchen. He walked rather stiffly down the narrow hallway and into the cluttered lounge once more, wishing at that moment that he was anywhere else but where he was. Even a visit to the dentist would have been preferable to what he was about to say.

He sat down in one of the overstuffed armchairs and watched while she closed the door behind her, then crossed her arms as she whirled to face him across the room.

'Don't think I'm impressed with the way you've wormed yourself into Sarah's affections just to get to me,' she snapped. 'You're a sneaky, conscienceless, manipulative devil, Luke St Clair, and I want nothing more to do with you.'

Luke scooped in a deep, steadying breath and let it out slowly as he reclined fully in the chair. There was no point in losing his temper—nothing to be gained by trading insults. But, damn it all, his heart was pounding away inside his chest and he was having a hard battle controlling his blood pressure. He planted both his hands firmly over the ends of the armrests, tipped his head back and locked eyes with her.

'I wish it were as simple as that, Rachel,' he began. 'I wish all that had brought me here was a desire to sample your delectable wares one more time. But that is not the case...'

'Really!' she snorted. 'Pardon me if I find that hard to believe. I've met your type before.'

'I doubt that, Rachel,' he replied coldly. 'I'm not a type. I'm an individual, with a mind of my own, a passion for the truth, and a stubbornness of spirit which only a mother can admire.'

'Charming. Now get to the point!'

'Very well.' The cords in Luke's neck stood out as he struggled for composure. 'I know Derek was born two months premature. I know your husband was ill with leukaemia for some time before he actually died. I suspect Derek is my child. What have you to say to that?'

Nothing.

That was what she had to say to that. She merely stared at him with pained eyes, then started shaking her head as though she could not believe that this was happening. Her arms unfolded and fell limply to her sides, her shoulders sagging in defeat.

'No,' she finally whispered. 'No...'

Turning, she clenched her hands into fists against the door, and was about to bang them on the wood when she stopped herself, spinning back to face him with a determined and tortured face. 'No,' she denied in a low, shaking voice, but with a firmness that had Luke leaping to his feet.

'What do you mean...*no*?' he demanded. 'You had unprotected sex with me seven months before Derek was born. Since he was born two months premature, even I can add seven and two and make nine. Even if you slept with dozens of other men around the same time, how can you be sure he's not mine?'

'There weren't dozens of other men,' she admitted at last in a strangled voice. 'The only person who could have been the father of my baby other than my husband was you. And you're quite right. I couldn't be sure, so I had DNA tests done after Derek was born. I know whose baby my son is, Luke, and you don't have to worry any more. He's not yours. He's a Cleary.'

Luke sank slowly down into the armchair, his eyes dropping blankly to the floor. He felt as if someone had just punched him in the stomach. Derek wasn't his. Rachel wasn't the mother of his baby. Everything he'd been secretly hoping and planning...poof! Out of the window.

'I can appreciate how relieved you must be,' Rachel said, the caustic note in her voice sending his eyes flashing up to find hers.

But she wasn't looking at him any more. She'd turned to stare at her wedding pictures on the wall, the action hurting Luke so much that it propelled him from self-pity into a simmering fury.

'So why did you do it?' he snarled. 'Just tell me that. Hell, I think I at least deserve an explanation.'

She turned slowly to set bitter eyes upon him. 'Do you, just? And why is that? You came with me that night without a second thought, Luke. And I'll bet you didn't give me a second thought the next morning either.'

'Then you'd be wrong, lover,' he snapped, jumping to his feet. 'I gave you plenty of thought while I worried my guts out for the next three months that I might have caught bloody AIDS!'

'Oh!' she cried, her remorseful expression seemingly real. 'So you did worry about that. I...I wondered afterwards. I *am* sorry for putting you through that, Luke. Truly.'

'Then why did you do it?' he demanded to know, his heart still aching from her disclosure. 'Tell me. I want...no, *need* to know. Hell, Rachel, would it hurt to tell me the whole truth? I can see now you're not some kind of slut, who'd make a habit of doing that sort of thing. But you were deliberately trying to get pregnant with me that night, weren't you? It wasn't some kind of crazy fling you were having, was it?'

'No,' came the husky admission. 'No, you're quite right. I was trying to get pregnant.' Tears filled her eyes and began falling silently down her cheeks. 'You'd never understand how it was, Luke. No man could ever understand...'

Her tears moved him deeply, but he wasn't about to back away. Only by knowing the whole truth could he begin to come to terms with the disappointment of Derek not being his.

'Try me, Rachel,' he choked out. 'I'm a good listener.'

Which was a lie, Luke realised, the moment the claim came out of his mouth. He'd never been a good listener. All his life he'd trodden a selfish path, where only *his* wishes mattered, only *his* desires and dreams. When had he ever stopped to really listen to anyone else's dreams or problems?

Bloody never.

Even now he wasn't wanting to listen for *her* sake, but to salve his own male ego.

This brutally honest self-realisation had him taking a good look at himself from Rachel's point of view. Hell, if she had a bad opinion of him then he only had himself to blame.

But all that was going to change, he vowed. As of right now.

'Even if I tell you everything,' she said, blinking away her tears, 'you'll never appreciate the situation at the time. No man could.'

'Rachel,' he said firmly. 'In another ten minutes Sarah will come back inside with Derek. Just give me the facts. I won't think the worst of you. Just tell me how it was, and what led you to taking such desperate measures.'

'And then you'll go?' she cried, her voice pleading.

'We'll see, Rachel.' Already his mind was shifting to other hopes, other dreams. Attainable ones.

He must have betrayed something of his secret desires, for her face hardened then. 'Don't go misunderstanding what happened last night, Luke,' she said sharply. 'It was a mistake, and one which I won't repeat. I know I gave the impression I was a sure thing where you're concerned, but that's not true any more. Believe me when I tell you I won't go to bed with you again. Never, ever. So you'd be wasting your time hanging around here.'

He believed that *she* believed what she was saying. So he let her believe it for the time being.

'Just tell me what happened, Rachel?'

His firm stance brought a wearily resigned sigh. 'All right, but I'm beyond dressing it up to make you feel sympathetic. I'm beyond caring what you think of me, anyway. I did it, and given the same circumstances I'd probably do it again. Not that that makes it right...'

Luke sat down while she stood there silently for a few seconds, her mind obviously off in the past. He waited impatiently for her to continue, and was about to say something when she launched into the explanation.

'I never knew my father,' she said, and Luke's head snapped back in the chair. Good God, she was going back a long way. But he remained silent, knowing that any further interruptions would only delay things.

'He died when I was only two. My mother was a wonderful woman, but inclined to be overprotective—especially when I grew up to be better than average-looking. She was afraid, you see, that I would become easy prey to the rich, handsome, conscienceless men of this world, who sought to use any pretty but naïve young woman who crossed their path. When I became a model I began to see what she meant. I *was* pursued by such men, and I fell prey to their empty charm a couple of times before I woke up to their lies. And my own silly self.'

Luke frowned at this, and might have said something if she hadn't immediately swept on with her story.

'By the time I met my future husband, at the ripe old age of twenty-two, I'd become somewhat wary of all super-good-looking men—rich or not. Patrick wasn't overly handsome or overly rich or overly anything. He was, however, a fascinating man, with a brilliant mind, who was already at the top of his scientific field at only thirty-four.

'We met at a benefit to raise money for research into congenital defects in children—his field. I fell in love with him, and when he asked me to quit modelling, marry him and have his children, I said yes like a shot. My mother was delighted—she'd begun to seriously worry about the direction of my life—and wished me every happiness as Mrs Patrick Cleary.'

Rachel's unhappy sigh led Luke to the astonishing thought that she had not found such great happiness as Mrs Patrick Cleary. Had this been due to his sickness, he wondered, or something else? Hadn't her brilliant husband turned out to be the Prince Charming she'd imagined him to be?

Not too many men, Luke reckoned, were saints. He would imagine that a man who had chosen scientific research as a career might be a very self-absorbed individual, a workaholic-type with little time put aside for the little wife at home.

But it was hardly the right time to suggest as much.

'A few weeks after our wedding,' Rachel said quietly, 'my mum died suddenly of a stroke. It...it was a big shock to me. She was only forty-nine. I found it difficult to come to terms with her death.

If it hadn't been for Sarah's sweet sympathy and kindness, I might have actually had a breakdown.

'She was a big comfort, too, when several months went by and I didn't fall pregnant. Patrick was most upset by this, and impossible to reason with. He was anxious to have children, and especially a son to carry on the family name. I told him that conceiving sometimes took time, but he insisted I went for every test in the book.

'When the news came back that I was fine, he finally consented to have tests done himself. He found out that his sperm count *was* a little low, but... worse... he was suffering from leukaemia—the same disease which had claimed his own father thirty years before.

'We were all devastated by the news. Patrick knew he had a long stint of chemotherapy ahead of him and, unbeknown to me, he had some of his sperm frozen and stored in the sperm bank of a large Sydney hospital. He had no intention, it seemed, of giving up his idea of having a son and heir.

'Meanwhile, he wasn't well enough for a normal sex life—although we did manage to make love every so often. Still, not enough to make conception a likelihood. He did go into a type of remission for a few short months, and we did resume marital relations on a regular basis, but still... no baby.

'When Patrick became ill again, and was diagnosed as terminal, he came up with the idea of my being artificially inseminated with his sperm every month. He had me take my temperature every morning before rising, and charted everything. Then, when my temperature dropped and it seemed ovulation was imminent, I would take the train up to Sydney, visit the hospital for the necessary procedure, spend the rest of that day and night resting in a hotel room, then return home the next day.

'I did this for five consecutive months, and every time...nothing. I began to dread getting my period and seeing the despair in Patrick's eyes. I would have done anything to stop him looking like that. The doctors said that if I could get pregnant he might find the will to last another couple of years, but I have to admit that I wanted a child myself. My life had become so lonely and so wretched, without focus or meaning. I needed something of my own to love and hold. It had been so long since Patrick had even touched me, let alone held me.'

Rachel faced him then, for the first time since she'd started talking. 'So I did what I did, God forgive me, thinking I was doing something noble. But from the moment you touched me, Luke, and held me and kissed me, I became caught up in something so different from what I'd originally intended. I won't lie and say I didn't enjoy every single moment I spent with you that night. I did. But believe me when I say I've suffered for my sin, Luke. I'm only sorry that I unwittingly made you suffer as well. I apologise deeply for that. I really do.'

'And you're absolutely sure of the child's parentage?' he asked thickly. 'There's no doubt?'

Rachel stiffened and drew herself up tall, as if in indignation that he would ask that question a second time. 'No doubt at all,' came her staunch reply. 'I'd been artificially inseminated with Patrick's sperm that same afternoon. I can only assume that my making love with you set off more normal processes within my body, which resulted in it being more conducive to conception.'

Luke couldn't help the grimace of distaste which flitted across his face.

'Yes, it's all very tacky, isn't it?' she snapped. 'Just like last night was tacky. I don't want to be tacky with you any more, Luke,' she said, her voice shaking with emotion. 'Enough is enough. Now I want you to go.' Again she crossed her arms, her expression and her stance carrying the message that this encounter was at an end.

He stood up slowly, that she was far too upset at that moment to accept anything from him at all. But he had no intention of leaving her alone. Either her or the boy. Derek might not be his child, but he could have been . . . oh, so easily.

As perverse as it might have seemed, it was enough for Luke. For some strange reason he didn't feel any different about the child for knowing he was not the biological father. His heart filled as he imagined what it would have been like to be such a child's *real* father—to love him and look after him. Luke liked the feeling it gave him. It felt right.

'I fully agree with you, Rachel,' he said quietly. 'I don't want there to be anything tacky between us any more either. *Au revoir*,' he said, and, nodding towards her stunned face, he swept past her, out into the hallway and out of the house.

Luke wasn't too sure what he was going to do, or how he was going to achieve his objectives. All he knew was that he was going to win that woman— that beautiful, brave, wonderful woman. Indeed, a woman worth loving!

CHAPTER ELEVEN

'FORGIVE me for asking,' his mother said to him over dinner that evening. 'But are you involved with a married woman?'

Luke's first reaction was a mixture of surprise and resentment at such a question. But seeing the real worry in his mother's eyes softened his attitude, and he decided—after a moment's hesitation—to tell her about Rachel and Derek. She would have to know eventually, anyway, because they were going to become part of his life. Luke wasn't sure how he was going to make that miracle come true, but make it come true, he would. Or die trying.

'So that's the story,' he finished over coffee. 'Now, before you open your mouth and put your foot in it, Mum,' he warned her, 'I want to add that I'm going to marry Rachel. Derek might not be mine, but it makes no difference. He's a grand little kid and needs a father. That father is going to be me!'

'But . . . but the mother doesn't want to have any more to do with you!'

Trust his own mother to come straight to the crux of his problem! 'Yes, do I realise that,' he tossed back, recklessly dismissing the niggling qualms which lurked deep within over Rachel's antagonism. 'But I aim to start overcoming that small hurdle in the near future.'

Somehow . . .

'How?' his mother asked, and Luke's pessimistic gut-feeling raised its ugly head again, filling him with exasperation.

'Must you be so negative? Look, I can't say I know, rightly. *Yet*. I'll sleep on it.' He carried his coffee-cup and saucer over to the sink. 'After I've helped my favourite girl with the washing-up, that is. This male chauvinist pig is going to have to turn over a new leaf if he's going to settle down to married bliss and family responsibilities.'

Grace rolled her eyes, stood up and carried her own half-full cup over to pour down the sink. 'You can't *make* her love you, Luke,' she said. 'Or marry you.'

'You think not?' he returned darkly. 'I have the advantage of certain admissions she once made to me. If all else fails, I will have to resort to desperation tactics.'

Grace stared at her son. She hoped he didn't mean what she thought he meant. Men who believed sex and seduction were the way to a woman's heart were fools! Lord, she hoped he wasn't planning on making her pregnant again. That would be a disaster!

'Mind if I make a suggestion, Luke?'

'Not as long as it's constructive.'

'You mentioned that you thought their house looked a bit shabby, and the yard unkempt. You might do something about that to start with.'

Luke frowned. 'You mean pay someone to fix it up?'

'Heavens, no. From the sound of things your Rachel would bitterly resent that. She sounds like a very proud lady. I was thinking more of you doing some work around the place yourself. You were pretty good with a mower and a paintbrush when you were a lad. The old mower in the garage still works. And there's a fairly new whipper-snipper Mark and Andy bought me last year, plus more paint than you can climb over. Those brothers of yours are always using *my* garage to store *their* leftovers. Serve them right if some of it goes missing.'

Luke's face broke into a wide smile, and Grace's heart turned over as he hugged her close. 'What a fantastic idea, Mum! I never would have thought of it. Thanks a million. I'll get started on "Project Cool Hand Luke" first thing in the morning. But let's hope I'm more successful than the original Cool Hand Luke. He died at the end of the movie. 'Night, Mum. Sleep tight.'

Grace went to bed, trying to feel optimistic about Luke's future with this woman, but it wasn't easy. She hoped it hadn't been just sexual frustration which had made this Rachel respond to Luke during that first torrid encounter and then again this week. She hoped that somehow, some way, his basic decency and good character had shone through his distracting sex appeal and had captured a little of her heart as well as her body.

Grace's thoughts finally turned to the boy who could quite easily have been her own grandchild.

What a shame, she thought, that the baby hadn't turned out to be Luke's. Patrick Cleary was dead now, so it wouldn't have mattered to him, and, as she'd always believed, Luke would have made a very good father.

He would still make a good father to the boy, Grace believed, if only the mother would give him a chance.

Let her give him a chance, Lord, Grace prayed as she drifted off to sleep. He really is a good man.

The house was empty when Luke turned up the following morning, and Luke panicked for a moment till he went round to the backyard and saw lots of toys still in the sandpit. Peering through the kitchen window, he also spied a few breakfast dishes in the sink. He couldn't imagine someone like Sarah being persuaded to abandon the house without doing the washing-up. She was of his mother's vintage, and such a wickedness would not be allowed.

Rachel, however, was another matter. Luke could well imagine her deserting the washing-up if she had other priorities for her time. Various X-rated thoughts zoomed into his head, and with a groan of frustration Luke spun away from the window. This would never do. He hadn't come back to bed her again, but to win her love.

Still, as he'd implied to his mother, he would use whatever weapons were at his disposal if failure was on the cards. For how could he simply walk away, when he knew that this was the woman he'd waited for all his life?

Two hours later the front and backyards had been transformed—the lawns mowed, the edges done, the garden beds weeded. But there was still no sight of the occupants.

Luke ran through the various possibilities in his head. They might have gone shopping, or to the doctor, or simply gone out for a drive. A glance at his watch showed eleven-thirty. One would think they wouldn't stay out too long with an eleven-month-old child. Derek would need a sleep soon, surely.

Hunger pangs reminded Luke that it had been a few hours since breakfast. He drank some water out of the hose, and was contemplating going back home for lunch when he heard a car throttling down out at the front. His heart was in his mouth as he hurried around the side of the house, relief flooding through him on seeing Rachel's car turn into the driveway and stop at the gates. He could see Sarah in the passenger seat and baby Derek perched up in a baby car-seat in the back.

Luke strode quickly down the pathway to open the gates, but Rachel was out of the car and there before him. The look she gave him was lethal.

'What in hell are you doing here?' she snapped under her breath as he drew near. 'And who in hell do you think you are, mowing my lawns without permission?'

'Morning, Rachel,' he returned coolly, totally ignoring her angry tirade. 'Been shopping, have you?' he said and waved at Sarah, who was smiling at him from the passenger seat, then at Derek, who was looking cranky. 'Now, don't make a scene in front of the family,' he whispered as he helped her open the gates.

'This isn't going to work, Luke,' she muttered. 'I want you to go away and stay away.'

He gave her a steely look. 'Don't be so bloody stupid. I care about you, Rachel, and I'm not going anywhere, so you might as well get used to me hanging around.'

'But... but you can't!'

'Can't what? Can't care about you? Why not? You're a lovely woman, with a lot more going for you than your looks, though you do seem to have a problem with your temper.'

'But you... you said you were going back to America,' she wailed.

'My plans have changed.'

'Oh, God...'

'There's no need to pray, Rachel. I have no intention of hurting you.'

'But you will. Don't you see?' she groaned. 'Every time I look at you it will hurt me.'

Sarah, unwinding the window and putting her head out, stopped that conversation dead in its tracks. 'Derek's beginning to grizzle, Rachel,' she called out.

'Coming,' Rachel said. 'We'll finish this later.'

'Over dinner tonight?'

Her eyes flashed fury at him.

'I'm not going to go away, Rachel.'

'Damn you, Luke. Why can't you be like all the others?' she threw at him, before whirling and striding back to the car, slamming the door as she climbed in and driving past him to park under the carport.

All the others?

Luke frowned his disgruntled puzzlement as he just stood there.

What others? Other lovers she'd had? Ones who'd loved and left her?

Damn it all. He hated to think of her with other men. It was hard enough coming to terms with her husband!

Derek's irritable cries snapped Luke out of his brooding reverie, although he was in no mood to be all sweetness and light as he strode over and yanked open the back door. He used brisk, somewhat brusque movements to unbuckle the child from his baby car-seat and whisk him out.

'Now, you stop that grizzling this instant, you little tyrant!' he ordered as he perched Derek firmly on his hip.

Derek's whingeing dried up immediately, a wide smile breaking over his cherubic face. His big glistening brown eyes twinkled cheekily as he reached up and started playing with a lock of Luke's hair which had fallen across his forehead. He even began making 'ga-ga' noises which sounded rather close to 'da-da'.

Luke couldn't help it. He was instantly entranced, a slave from that moment onward.

'See, Rachel?' Sarah said. 'That's just what Derek needs occasionally. A firm male hand. Look, he's being as good as gold for Luke.'

'In that case Luke can mind the little devil for the rest of the afternoon,' she retorted as she gathered up several bags of groceries from the car and set off towards the house. 'I suppose you'd better invite the Good Samaritan in for lunch, Sarah,' she called back over her shoulder in waspish tones. 'No doubt he'll expect some payment for all his work,' she finished drily.

Sarah sent Luke an apologetic shrug. 'It's been a trying morning,' she whispered. 'I'd better go and open the back door for Rachel before she drops all the shopping. *Again*,' she added meaningfully before hurrying off.

Derek immediately blotted his copybook by bursting into loud cries the moment his grand-mother disappeared.

'I can see where you get your sweet tem-perament,' he told the bawling infant as he walked him round the yard, trying to get him to stop crying. But to no avail.

Sarah popped her head out of the back door. 'Better bring him inside, Luke. The poor love's tired and hungry and needs his nappy changed.'

The poor love created merry hell till Rachel took him off to bed. Luke had by then finished the last of the two huge sandwiches Sarah had made him, and he put down his mug of coffee with a relieved sigh at the sudden blessed silence. 'My God, is he always as bad as that?' he asked.

'Heavens, no. He's just overtired from our shopping expedition. He should have been in bed at ten for his morning nap. Any other child would have just dropped off in his stroller, but not Derek. He finds looking around in the mall far too interesting to go to sleep. Same thing in the car. Most babies drift off during a drive, but never Derek. He likes looking around too much.'

'Mum says I was like that,' Luke remarked. 'I was a bad sleeper too. Never lasted longer than four hours at a time. Apparently my bedroom was filled with different coloured lamps, and the whole ceiling was covered in colourful mobiles because it was the only way Mum could get some rest. I used to lie there for hours just watching the shapes move and the light play on the various surfaces.'

'Maybe that's why you became a photographer?' Sarah suggested.

'You could be right. I never connected the two things before. How clever of you, Sarah. Speaking of photography, I'd like to take some shots of Derek later. I have a few frames left in a roll I have in a camera in the car, and I might as well use them up before I get the roll developed.'

'Oh, that would be wonderful. We really haven't got all that many photos of him. As I'm sure you've gathered, money's a bit tight. Patrick's illness used up all his savings, and then some more. After he died we found out he'd taken a second mortgage on the house. Naturally he hadn't earned any salary for ages. He lost his position with the international drug company he'd been doing research for soon after he was diagnosed with cancer. They treated him shamefully. Quite shamefully.'

'Do you own this place?'

'Oh, no. There's no money left at all. We rent. For a while after Patrick died we both got by, by pooling our social security cheques. But Rachel realised that wasn't going to be enough when Derek got older so she decided to go back to work. She's been doing quite well too, getting more and more work all the time.'

'She's a very good model.'

'And very beautiful,' Sarah added, managing to put a questioning note into the words and worry into her glance at Luke.

He smiled a reassuring smile. 'I can see I'm not going to be able to put anything over on you, Sarah. Yes, my interest in Rachel is more than professional, but my intentions are honourable. The only trouble around here will be convincing Rachel of that.'

'She...she did love Patrick very much,' Sarah said hesitantly. 'She's been through a lot.'

'Yes,' was all he said.

Sarah sighed. 'But life goes on, doesn't it? I mean...she's only a young woman, and it's silly to think there won't be another man for her one day. If...if that man turns out to be you, Luke, then I for one couldn't be happier.'

Luke reached across the table to squeeze Sarah's hand. 'Thank you. I appreciate that. Do you think you might talk her into going out to dinner with me tonight?'

'You mean she's refused?' Sarah's surprise was both flattering and encouraging.

'Uh-huh.'

'Don't take it personally, Luke. She probably just doesn't want to ask me to mind Derek again. Which is so silly, really. I love minding him, and he's usually quite good at night. The other night was an exception. Now that we have that stuff for his gums, it'll be plain sailing.'

'I'll play with him when he wakes up later and tire him right out,' Luke suggested enthusiastically.

Sarah laughed. 'What a good idea! And you can take those photographs while you're at it.'

'What photographs?' Rachel asked as she walked back into the room, casting a suspicious glare at Luke.

'Of Derek,' Sarah answered. 'Luke's going to take a few snapshots and give them to us. Isn't that nice of him?'

'Yes,' came the taut reply. 'Very nice.'

'I assured him I don't mind minding Derek while you two young ones go out to dinner tonight.'

Rachel's smile was brittle. 'That's sweet of you, Sarah, but I really can't accept.'

'Nonsense. I insist.'

'And so do I,' Luke piped up. 'I think it's the least you can do to repay me for all the work I've done around here today. I haven't finished either. I thought I'd slap some paint on the carport. The posts are beginning to weather badly.'

Rachel looked from one to the other, then sighed and smiled sweetly. 'I can see I've been successfully outmanoeuvred. All right. Dinner tonight it is. Luke, can I see you outside for a minute? I'd like to see exactly what colour paint you're going to use. The landlord might not appreciate a pink carport.'

Any air of sweet acquiescence disappeared the second she was alone with him. 'Now, you listen here, Luke St Clair,' she spat, poking him in the chest with a very angry finger. 'I told you once and now I'm telling you again. I will not have you conning poor Sarah just to get to me. Neither will I have you blatantly using my son for the same reasons. I know exactly what you want, and it isn't just an innocent dinner-date!'

'True.'

'Ahh, so you finally admit it!' She folded her arms and glared up at him, looking incredibly beautiful with her cheeks all flushed and her green eyes flashing with anger.

'That depends. Exactly what am I supposed to be admitting to?'

'That the only reason you're . . . hanging around, as you so delicately put it earlier . . . is because you think I'm a sure thing where you're concerned.'

'Which you are,' he muttered, surprising her and himself by suddenly grabbing her shoulders and yanking her hard against him.

But, dear heaven, there was only so much pushing a man could take. Having gone this far, Luke didn't give her enough time to do more than gasp with shock before his mouth covered hers and his tongue was driving deep between her startled lips.

She didn't disappoint him.

God, no. She wouldn't be so bloody merciful!

It was the same as it had always been, once she was in his arms and being thoroughly kissed, every muscle in her body freezing for a few tantalising seconds before melting against him in one deliciously submissive wave of surrender. The feeling of power it sent crashing through Luke's veins was so intoxicating that he wondered momentarily if this *was* all he wanted of her. Hell, she made him feel more of a man than any woman he'd ever known.

Yet she was in no way a weak woman.

Till she was in his arms.

Then she *was* weak.

He broke from her mouth and she gazed up at him with anguished green eyes. 'You bastard,' she cried, even while she still clung to him. 'Why can't you leave me alone?'

'Because you don't want me to,' he returned thickly, then kissed her again—kissed her till she was jelly-kneed and trembling. Luke himself wasn't feeling too calm either, the state of his body routing all his earlier good intentions.

'We must stop,' she moaned, after the kissing had gone on for even more minutes, by which time Luke was in danger of spontaneous combustion.

It crossed his mind to push her round to the side of the house right now, or into the back of her car, and just do it, like two hormone-crazed teenagers. But it was stark daylight, and Sarah might come looking for them at any second.

Thinking of Sarah brought Luke back to earth with a jolt. Hell, what was he doing, letting the heat of the moment reduce his feelings for Rachel to nothing but lust? Clearly she expected a little more of him, and it was up to him to prove otherwise to her.

Dammit, he wasn't handling this encounter at all well!

'You're right,' he said abruptly, after tearing his mouth away from hers again. 'This isn't at all what I want.' His arms dropped back to his sides and he took a backward step, putting some distance between himself and the heat of her softly lush curves.

Her face remained flushed, but her mouth took on a cynical twist as her gaze swept down to where his tight jeans hid nothing of his stark arousal.

'Oh, I don't doubt that,' she said caustically. 'Men like you want it all, yet in reality you want nothing of value!'

'You're wrong, Rachel. Wrong about me and wrong about what I want.'

'Am I?' she jeered. 'Well, we'll see tonight, won't we, who's right and who's wrong? I'm sure you won't surprise me.'

Luke dragged in then let out a shuddering sigh. 'Look, we could keep trading insults all afternoon, but it won't prove anything. I'll let my actions speak for me tonight.'

'Like your actions spoke for you a few moments ago?' she scorned. 'Well, they do say actions speak louder than words.'

Luke's teeth clenched down hard in his jaw. Geez, but she would try the patience of a saint. It was no wonder he'd ended up kissing her. It was the only way to shut that smart mouth of hers.

'If you're so sure of my shallow character and intentions,' he pointed out testily, 'then why are you going out with me tonight at all?'

'Why, indeed?' she said in a self-mocking tone. 'Maybe I'm a masochist. Or maybe I just like to live dangerously.'

'Or maybe you like me a whole lot more than you care to admit!'

Her reaction to his ground out remark was a familiar one.

Fear.

It totally exasperated Luke.

'For pity's sake, Rachel, why do you have to look like that?' he groaned. 'How many times do I have to tell that I won't hurt you?'

'And how many times do I have to tell *you* that you will—by just being *you*!' she countered, any fear quickly changing to a heart-wrenching sadness. 'As for pity...why don't you take pity on me and just go away? Can't you see that's what I really want? What do I have to do to make you go away and stay away?'

'A while back you said actions spoke louder than words, Rachel. Well, you're right!' Quite ruthlessly, he scooped an arm around her waist and drew her hard against him, cupping her chin with his other hand while he took her mouth in a brief but hungry kiss.

It was enough for her lips to quiver and her eyes to dilate wildly. 'When you stop responding to my kisses the way you do,' he rasped, 'then and only then will I go away and stay away. Now I want *you* to go away. Temporarily. I think I need a break from your hating me so much.'

She looked up at him with hurt eyes, but he felt no mercy at that point in time. He suspected that he would have little mercy for her tonight either, if things turned bad. Her fierce desire for him was the only weapon he had left, and if needs be he would use it.

She knew it too. Which was perhaps why she was looking at him the way she was. With real hatred this time.

'Men like you should be drowned at birth,' she snapped, and, whirling, sailed off towards the back door.

But the message her bejeaned bottom sent back to Luke as it swayed seductively from side to side was totally at odds with what she'd just said. Luke smiled a devilish smile, then set about painting the carport, whistling as he worked.

CHAPTER TWELVE

'SO HOW did it go?' Grace asked Luke the moment he walked in the door. She'd been on tenterhooks all day, wondering and worrying about him.

He waved his hand in a so-so gesture. 'I'll know more after tonight. I'm taking her out to dinner.'

'Where?'

'Just a small seafood restaurant. Nowhere extra fancy. She wouldn't like that. She'd only think I was trying to impress her. Or seduce her.'

The bitter tone in that last remark bothered Grace, till she put two and two together and came up with a very obvious four. 'She thinks you only want an affair, doesn't she?'

'Something like that.'

Looking at Luke, Grace could appreciate that. Did he have any idea how handsome and sexy a man he was? She was his mother, and she could see it. How much more would a young attractive woman?

'What did she think of your mowing her lawns?'

'She thought it was all a ploy to get her into bed. She even thinks the same about my being nice to the boy.'

'You'll just have to hang in there, Luke, and prove her wrong. Time should do that. Meanwhile, try to keep your hands off.'

'Would it were that simple,' he muttered. 'Mum, could you iron me a shirt while I have a shower? I have to hurry.'

'But it's only five past five. When do you have to pick her up?'

'Seven. But I've a bit of shopping I'd like to do first. And I have to drop by at Theo's on the way. I left some rolls of film with him to be developed, and he's doing them for me straight away.'

'Are they the photos you took of Rachel in bikinis?'

'Yes, but it's not them that the hurry's for. I took a few snaps of Derek this afternoon, playing in his sandpit, which I thought might turn out rather well, and I wanted to give them to Rachel tonight.'

'Oh, I'd love to see them too. Have Theo run off an extra copy of them for me, will you? Actually, I wouldn't mind having a peek at the ones of Rachel too.'

'Sticky-beak. No worry. He's doing two of everything as a matter of course. Now, how about ironing that shirt? I'd do it, but you do it so much better.'

'Flatterer. Which one?'

'The black silk.'

Grace gave him a sharp look. 'Don't you think another shirt would be a wiser choice? Why not your cream one? Or that lovely blue lawn one with the stitched down pocket?'

'The black silk,' he repeated stubbornly.

Grace heaved a resigned sigh. 'You're still trying to get to her through sex, Luke, and it's not the right way.'

'Agreed. But it might end up being the only way. And if it is, I'm going to take it.'

Grace shook her head, her heart full of real fear for Luke's future. But she knew there was no arguing with him. He would simply clean up, then iron his own damned shirt.

She cluck-clucked her tongue in utter exasperation as she walked out to the laundry and drew the aforementioned garment out of the clothes basket, glaring at it as she spread it out on the ironing-board. He looked as handsome as the devil in that shirt, and wickedly sexy.

Poor Rachel, she thought.

And poor Luke.

The man simply had no idea. Women with babies didn't want just sex. Not without security in tow. And Luke in that shirt represented only the former.

But he would have to learn the bitter lessons of life for himself, wouldn't he? Maybe next time he'd listen to his mother!

'Wow, wow, and triple wow!' was Theo's greeting to Luke when he dropped by to pick up the photos. 'Now I understand. I'd fall in love with her myself if you hadn't got there first.'

'Thanks, Theo,' Luke returned, with a wry smile as he took the large brown envelopes. 'I take it your little beauties performed well?'

'You'd take great pictures with a box Brownie, Luke. If you weren't such a good mate I'd be filthy jealous. I take it you're off to see the gorgeous blonde in the bikini?' he said, casting a rueful eye over Luke's appearance.

'Yes, and I'm running late.' Luke had taken simply ages in the baby shop, selecting mobiles for Derek's room.

'Off you go, then. Far be it from me to stand in the way of true love. Oh, by the way, who's the kid? The one with eyes you could drown in.'

'That's Derek. He belongs to the gorgeous blonde in the bikini.'

'Really? Would I be out of line asking if you're the father?'

Luke's chest contracted. He wished.

'No, I'm not,' he said brusquely.

'Then, who is?'

'Her husband.'

'Oh, hell.'

'Not quite. She's a widow.'

Theo still wrinkled his nose at the situation. 'Not good, man. I wouldn't raise another man's kid. Not even if the mother *was* a golden goddess. Give it ten years or so, man, and the kid'll be telling you to get lost, and not to tell him what to do 'cause you're not his *real* father.'

'But I *will* be his real father, Theo. I'm going to adopt him. Now, I must go. We'll go out for drinks some time shortly, right?'

'Only if I can be best man at the wedding.'

'You're on!'

Theo's words stayed with Luke during the drive down to Rachel's place. He could see the sense in his friend's warning, but somehow it didn't seem to apply to his relationship with Derek. When Luke looked at that kid, and held him and played with him, he felt a bonding which transcended biological fatherhood. It was an emotional thing which could not be analysed. He loved the child as surely as he loved the mother.

He even loved the grandmother too, in a way. They were a grand trio, and he wanted quite desperately to make life good for them again, to buy them all a beautiful big house, to lavish some luxuries on them to make up for the hard times they'd had before and since Patrick Cleary's death.

Luke thought of the mobiles he'd bought Derek and smiled. He'd love the dancing elephant one. Kids always liked elephants. The butterfly one was cute too. Then there was the racing car one, and last but not least the fairies. God, he hoped buying a boy a fairy mobile wouldn't be looked askance upon by Sarah or Rachel. It had been the most colourful—the fairies having luminescent wings which glowed in the dark.

When Luke stopped at the next set of red lights, he snatched up the brown envelope lying on the passenger seat, ripped open the flap and slid out the thick bundle of coloured prints.

Derek's were on top, and Luke could see what Theo had meant. His eyes were incredibly expressive—big, liquid brown pools. There again, the photographs were excellent too.

'Must have had a good photographer,' Luke said to himself, smiling.

Damn, but he was a cute kid!

Luke finally moved on to look at the shots of Rachel, and they quite blew him away. She was beautiful enough in the flesh, but on film she was something else. Again, it was in the eyes, he realised. They seemed to follow you, their expressions vivid, bringing to vibrant life a wide range of emotions, not to mention her sexuality and sensuality. No man could have looked at them and not wanted her. It was as simple as that.

He wanted her. Not for a day, or a night, but for always. He would marry her tomorrow if she would have him.

The horn blowing behind him reminded Luke that the lights had turned green. Throwing down the bundle of photos onto the seat, he accelerated off, the thought coming that maybe if he told Rachel he loved her straight off the bat, if he asked her to marry him, then she would know how serious he was.

OK, so she might not love him back. Yet. But she did desire him, and it wasn't such a big step, surely, from desire to love. He could also start letting her know how damned well-off he was— anything to sway her opinion of him as a heartless womaniser to a serious suitor of depth and standing.

It wasn't till he was standing on the front porch and ringing Rachel's doorbell that Luke remembered the black silk shirt and his mother's disapproval of it. He was frowning as Rachel opened the door, at which point his own appearance immediately ran a poor second to hers.

Dear Lord, but she was exquisite—breathtakingly so in that classically cut cream suit, her hair up and pearls at her ears and throat. A second, closer inspection revealed that the suit was far from new and the pearls only cheap imitations, but neither observation detracted from her beauty, or his admiration of her. In fact, he admired her all the more—for she had an inner beauty as well, born of an inner pride and strength of character.

'Hello, Rachel,' he said simply. 'You look lovely.'

'You're late,' she reprimanded him tautly.

'Only fifteen minutes.'

'I . . . I thought you weren't coming.'

Luke saw that her knuckles were white within the clenched fists at her sides. It was as telling as the tension in her voice.

'And I thought you wanted me to go away and stay away,' he returned drily.

She gave him a look which had a disturbingly strained edge to it.

Luke decided that some defusing was called for. 'I had some shopping to do,' he explained. 'For Derek.'

'For Derek?' Her tension moved up a notch, if anything.

'Yes. Some mobiles for his room. Would we have time to put one up, do you think?'

'You . . . you bought Derek some mobiles?'

'Yes. There's this elephant one which I'm dying to put up. I was telling Sarah earlier today how I

was a difficult baby too, and how Mum found that
mobiles hanging from my ceiling used to amuse me
for hours when I wouldn't sleep. I think they might
help with Derek. Can I come in and do the
honours? Don't tell me the little devil is asleep at
this early hour.'

Luke was startled when Rachel abruptly burst
into tears. 'Oh, God,' she sobbed, covering her face
with her hands. 'God...'

Luke didn't know what to do. 'Rachel...
darling...' He came inside, closing the door behind
him and propped the large parcel from the baby
shop against the door before taking her in his arms.
'What did I say? What's the matter? It's not Derek,
is it? He's all right, isn't he?'

Sarah came hurrying down the hall. 'What is it?'
she asked anxiously. 'What's wrong?'

Luke's bewilderment must have shown on his face
and in his voice. 'I don't know. I...I think my
buying Derek some mobiles upset her.'

Rachel began crying all the harder, sobbing into
his shirtfront. Luke threw Sarah a desperate look.

'Rachel, dear,' Sarah soothed, prying her away
from Luke's rapidly soaking shirt and leading her
distressed daughter-in-law back down the hall.
'You're going to make yourself sick, crying like this.
Now, why don't you have a little lie-down and—?'

'Make him go away,' she choked out, throwing
a wild-eyed and tortured glance over her shoulder
at Luke. 'I want him to go away. I can't stand the
sight of him any longer. I can't, I tell you.'

Luke felt himself go cold all over.

'Rachel!' Sarah exclaimed, utterly shocked.

'I've told him and told him, but he just won'
listen!' Rachel ranted hysterically. 'I don't want hir
in my life any more, but I don't have the strengt
to send him away! You have to do it for me, Sarah
before I do something dreadful. It's all become to
much. The guilt and the pain. I can't bear any mor
guilt...or any more pain. Please, Sarah,' she cried
'Make him go away.' And she collapsed against th
older woman, sobbing piteously.

'Rachel...dear...I...I don't know what you'r
talking about. Do...do you know what she's talkin
about, Luke?'

'Yes,' he said bitterly.

'Perhaps if you told me I could—'

'No, don't!' Rachel wailed, her ravaged fac
jerking up to plead with him far more eloquentl
than any words. 'Please, Luke,' she begged
hoarsely. 'Just go...'

Luke stared at her, and he saw the truth clearl
for the first time.

She would never get over what she had don
eighteen months ago. Never!

Technically she was an adulteress who had en
joyed her adultery, and she despised herself for it
Sarah had told him how much Rachel had loved
Patrick, so the guilt had to have been enormous a
the time—and long afterwards. As much as Rache
might still desire him, Luke, he would always be
the symbol of her guilt and her shame. She had
momentarily given in to the temptation of having
what she'd thought was another one-night stand

with him the other night, and then, when he'd followed her, she'd toyed with the idea of having a temporary affair with him.

But a lasting relationship had never been on the cards.

By buying her son such a personal present he'd crossed the line she'd made for him in her mind, and now there was nowhere for Luke to go except out of her life forever. He took one hard look at her dangerously distraught self, saw what his presence was doing to the woman he loved, and made the most difficult decision he had ever made in his life.

'It's all right, Rachel,' he said quietly, unaware that the pain in his face was more than a match for hers. 'I'll do what you want. I'll go. And you don't have to worry. I won't be back. Goodbye, Sarah. It's been a pleasure knowing you.'

He bent and picked up the package of mobiles, then handed it towards a white-faced Rachel. 'There's no reason why Derek can't enjoy these, is there? I mean . . . he doesn't ever have to know who they're from?'

When Rachel choked out another strangled sob, Luke shoved the mobiles into her arms, then spun away so that he didn't have to look upon her any more. He bit out a curt goodbye as he strode stiffly down the hall to let himself out, not looking back once.

Seeing the packet of photos on the passenger seat almost broke his iron composure, and only by sheer will power did Luke start that damned car and drive off. He kept a tight rein on his feelings all the way home, putting himself into a traffic-induced trance, thinking of nothing but getting from point A to point B.

Impossible, though, to maintain his stoic façade once he came face to face with his mother, with her puzzled questions and gently concerned face. He could feel himself dissolving inside as he explained rather curtly that it was over between himself and Rachel.

'But... But...'

'No buts, Mum. Just over. She doesn't want to see me any more. To use her exact words—she can't stand the sight of me!'

Luke knew he had to get out of his mother's presence before he embarrassed himself totally. Hell, any moment now he'd be blubbering like an idiot!

Steeling his ominously quivering chin, he tossed the envelope full of photographs on the kitchen table and stalked off towards his bedroom. 'Burn them once you've satisfied your curiosity,' he snarled over his shoulder. 'I couldn't bear to set eyes on *her* again either.'

CHAPTER THIRTEEN

GRACE shuddered at the slamming of Luke's bedroom door. She wasn't fooled by his display of temper, knowing full well that it was just a cover for a deep, deep hurt. If he'd been twelve, instead of thirty-two, she might have gone after him, taken him in her arms and tried to comfort him. Instead, all she could realistically do was give him some space.

Her eyes went to the envelope lying on the table, her curiosity very definitely piqued now. Grace sat down and poured the photos out of the open flap onto the table. She picked up the first two, her eyes going from one to the other.

What she saw was an extraordinarily beautiful girl, whose sex appeal rivalled Luke's. It fairly leapt out at one. But she had more than that, Grace appreciated. There was a strength of character in that lovely face which bespoke that she'd been through a lot, this Rachel. She was no little blonde dollybird. She was a woman in every sense of the word.

Grace studied each photograph in turn, noting with maternal pride that it wasn't just the model who was spectacular. The photographs themselves were breathtaking—especially the panoramic shots of the beaches and coastline. It would be a wicked shame to burn such art!

She began dividing the photographs into the ones which included Rachel and the ones which didn't. The former she would gladly burn. She was down to the last half-dozen prints before she came across the first one of the boy.

Grace blinked her shock, then quickly glanced at the others. Slowly, and with shaking hands, she spread the portraits of the laughing child out in front of her and just stared at them. Stared and stared and stared.

After a good ten minutes of staring, she rose and went in search of the family albums she kept in the bottom of the hall cupboard. And it was while she was kneeling there, extracting the oldest and largest of the albums, that she heard sounds coming from Luke's nearby bedroom which tore great holes in her mother's heart.

Her son was crying. Her thirty-two-year-old adult son was weeping as she was sure he hadn't wept in twenty years. Grace could remember well the last time he'd broken down this way. His pet dog—a big old Labrador that his father had bought when he was born and which had been Luke's constant companion since—had just been run over and killed.

Tears welled up in her own eyes as she recalled her son's heartbreak that day, as well as the hardness which had gradually replaced the tears. He'd vowed two things that day: never to have another dog, and never to waste his time crying over something, because it never did any good. His dog was dead and was going to stay dead—tears or no tears.

Grace knew that only total despair would have made Luke weep as he was weeping at this very moment. His hoarsely muffled sobs were just breaking her heart. Anger consumed her at this Rachel. Who did she think she was to play with her Luke's life like that? To ruthlessly use him as she had—not once, but twice—then toss him away?

The urge to burst into her son's room and tell him what she suspected about the boy's parentage was acute, but then she began to wonder if Luke already knew the awful truth—if that was the reason he was so distraught. She didn't know what to do then.

Grace decided to do what she usually did when faced with a stiff decision. She would put on the television and have a glass of sherry. Maybe even *two* glasses of sherry. Then, when she'd calmed down and Luke had calmed down, she might know what to do for the best.

Nearly forty minutes later, Grace was sitting in her favourite chair in the front room, mindlessly watching a movie on television and sipping the dregs of her second sherry, when the front doorbell rang. A frowning glance at the clock on the wall showed a quarter past nine. A little late for callers.

Shrugging, she levered herself out of the deep armchair, placed her glass down on a side-table and padded out to answer the front door.

Seeing Rachel in the photograph hadn't quite prepared Grace for seeing her in the flesh. The girl

was so fair and so tall! And so incredibly lovely
Even red-rimmed eyes and a general air of distress
didn't destroy her quite extraordinary beauty.

'Mrs St Clair?' she asked straight away, her voice
soft and shaky.

'That's correct,' Grace returned stiffly, not feeling
too kindly disposed towards her visitor.

'Is ... is Luke here?'

Grace's chin lifted. 'He is,' she returned coldly.
'You're Rachel, aren't you?'

'Yes. Yes, I'm Rachel,' she admitted rather
bleakly, as though she wasn't too proud of herself.

And rightly so too, Grace thought sourly.
Beautiful is as beautiful does!

'I must see him, Mrs St Clair,' Rachel pleaded.
'Please ... It ... it's very important.'

It was difficult not to be touched by the girl's
distress. But Grace wasn't prepared to make it easy
on her. 'Well, I don't know,' she said. 'I'm not sure
Luke will want to see you. He's very upset.'

'Oh, but I must see him! You don't understand.
I have something very, very important to tell him.'

'I think I understand only too well, Rachel. I've
seen the photographs Luke took of your boy. He
bears an amazing resemblance to his father at the
same age.'

Shocked green eyes confirmed what Grace had
been thinking for the past hour. 'Oh, God,' Rachel
groaned. 'He ... he hasn't guessed too, has he? You
didn't tell him what you ... you ... ?'

'No,' Grace denied. 'He hasn't guessed as far as
I know.'

'Then, please, Mrs St Clair, let me be the one to tell him. It has to come from me—don't you see?'

Grace could see the sense of that. 'I suppose so. But let me warn you, I won't have my son being used by you again. He's a good man, and he deserves better than the way you've treated him.'

'Yes, I know,' the girl said wretchedly. 'My behaviour has been inexcusable. All I can do is try to make things right now. Please... let me go to him...'

'You haven't changed your mind about this because you've found out Luke's a very rich, very successful man, have you?'

Again, her shocked green eyes told their own story. Lord, but the girl did have expressive eyes. 'No, no, I can see you haven't,' Grace muttered. 'Come along, then. I'll take you to him.'

Luke was sprawled across his bed, face-down, feeling nothing but a deep emotional exhaustion. Women claimed to feel better after they'd wept. From Luke's experience, men only felt more wretched. Weeping weakened a man's resolves and undermined his inner strength. He hadn't succumbed to it in twenty years, and it would be another damned twenty years before he succumbed again.

He was lying there thinking black thoughts when the front doorbell rang and his mother went to answer it. One of her cronies, he supposed, then turned his mind to other things. He would go back to America. Put some distance between himself and Rachel. It was the only way he could guarantee that he wouldn't give in to the temptation to see her again. It would be hell, but he would endure.

His mother's timid tapping on his bedroom door irritated him. Why couldn't she just leave him alone? Surely she could see that he wanted to be alone?

Well, not really. He wanted to be with Rachel. What he wouldn't give for her to walk into this room right this minute, throw her arms around him and tell him that she loved him . . .

Geez, what was he—a masochist? That wasn't going to happen. Not ever!

'What?' he snapped, when the tap-tap came again.

'You have a visitor, Luke,' his mother said.

Luke's heart jumped into his mouth. He sat bolt-upright and swung his legs over the side of the bed, staring wildly as the door opened. No, it couldn't be. It simply couldn't be.

Yet there she was, standing alone in the open doorway, staring back at him, his mother nowhere in sight.

Once he accepted that Rachel was real, and not some cruel figment of his imagination, a torrent of emotions raged through him—not the least of which was fury.

'What in hell are you doing here?' he snarled. 'Haven't you turned the screw enough yet? Or have you decided you want some more screwing for yourself? Is that it, Rachel? Is sex worth a little more guilt and shame? Hell, woman, don't just stand there, if that's the case. Get in here and get your gear off!'

She stunned him by walking in and actually shutting the door, though her expression was full of pain, not passion. 'You have every right to be angry with me, Luke. So I'll try not to be hurt by what you're saying. In a way, it's very telling of you to be so mad at me. I'll take some comfort from that.'

'Then don't! I think you're a right royal bitch, and if I ever see you again after tonight, it'll be too soon!'

'You don't mean that, Luke. I know you don't mean it.'

'And how in hell do you know that, pray tell?' he scorned, even while he recognised the truth of it. Man, he had to be the biggest fool of all time! She'd already shot him right between the eyes— metaphorically speaking—and he was lining up to be shot again.

'Sarah told me so. She also told me that you loved me, that you genuinely cared for Derek too, and that you probably wanted to marry me and make a family.'

'No kidding? And you couldn't see any of that for yourself? You needed an independent party to tell you what had to be bloody obvious to anyone with half a brain?'

Her face twisted into an anguished expression. 'Yes. Yes, I needed an independent party to tell me, because I've long ceased to be able to think straight where you're concerned, Luke. I stopped thinking straight about you the moment I saw you...eighteen months ago...at that exhibition.'

Luke felt his mouth go instantly dry. He stared at her, not daring to hope, but hoping all the same. He swallowed convulsively, and, when that didn't work, noisily cleared his throat. 'Don't go saying anything that isn't true, Rachel,' he choked out. 'If you do, I won't be responsible for what I might do.'

'I'm done with anything but the truth, Luke. It has to be the whole truth and nothing but the truth from now on.'

Tears shimmered in her eyes, and he was afraid. Afraid of what she was going to say, and afraid of how he might react.

'Go on,' he said tautly.

'I came to that exhibition in a state of utter desperation. I could no longer bear my existence at home—the way Patrick looked every month when my period came, plus my own awful loneliness. Sarah didn't live with us then, and Patrick had never been the husband I thought he would be. There was no real partnership between us—no sharing or companionship. He had his work and I...I had nothing.

'Oh, I'd been quite happy to give up my modelling to become a full-time wife and mother, because I was in love with Patrick, but when I didn't conceive straight away, his attitude changed towards me.

'Gradually I began to see that he'd married me not so much for love but because I was the perfect genetic specimen to be the mother of his children.

I was, in reality, a type of experiment—an incubator for the child who was to inherit the best of both of us. Brains *and* beauty.

'Of course, I didn't see all this at first—the penny not dropping till well after I'd become pregnant with Derek. But I was confused and hurt at how my marriage was turning out. I blamed my discontent on my failure to conceive and I placed all my energies on succeeding with that, ignoring the fact that I no longer loved my husband as I should have.

'In a way, I was relieved when he couldn't make love to me any more. I had long ceased to find any real pleasure in it, only guilt. Not that I liked being artificially inseminated either. But I imagined that if I gave Patrick the child he wanted he would be happy again, and *I* would be happy again too.

'My failure to conceive month after month began affecting my emotional and mental state. I was very depressed and decidedly unstable the night I decided to dress up like some kind of whore and seduce the first brown-eyed man I came across. Nothing mattered but conceiving a baby.'

Luke's heart twisted at her words. Was that all he'd been to her? A brown-eyed man? Hell...

'It never crossed my mind that I might be totally bewitched by that brown-eyed man,' she went on, green eyes glistening. 'That from the moment he took me in his arms, I'd belong to that brown-eyed man—not for just that night but for the rest of my life...'

Luke rose slowly to his feet, his heart beginning to thud heavily in his chest.

'I don't know if I fell in love with you that night, Luke,' she confessed. 'All I know is that afterwards I couldn't forget you. You haunted my thoughts every day and my dreams every night. Oh, the tears I cried over you. When you walked down that staircase the other morning, I nearly died. I didn't know what to do. When it seemed you didn't recognise me I *was* relieved at first, but then I was overwhelmed with the same feelings I'd felt that first night. God, how I wanted you!'

A tremor raced through Luke at the passion in her voice. But was she admitting to love? Or just lust? And when was she going to get back to the guilt which had crippled her, and their burgeoning relationship?

'God knows how I got through that day,' she said with an expressive shudder. 'What happened that night...I have no excuse for. I was mad with wanting you, Luke. I tried telling myself it was only sex, that afterwards I'd feel differently. But if anything I wanted you more than ever. I ran from you at the first excuse I could find, and when you came after me in the end I was forced to accept my true feelings for you.'

'Which are?' he asked, and held his breath.

'I love you, Luke. Love you,' she repeated croakily, then burst into tears again.

He groaned, then held his arms out to her. She ran into them and he clasped her to him, pressing his lips into her hair while he battled for control over his own heaving emotions. He kept a tight hold on her and himself till her sobs had subsided to shudders. When only the occasional quavering sigh whispered from her lungs, he held her out at arm's length.

'Then why, Rachel?' he asked, still not fully understanding. 'Why did you send me away? Why did you act as you did?'

'Promise me you won't hate me,' she cried softly. 'Promise me you'll try to understand.'

'I promise,' he said sincerely, knowing that nothing could ever make him hate her.

'Derek's yours, Luke,' came the shocking admission. 'I lied about the DNA test. Oh, yes, I got one done all right—after Patrick died. The hospital still had some of his frozen sperm samples. The child wasn't his, Luke. He had to be yours.'

Luke couldn't help it. Shock sent his arms dropping away from her as he took a staggered step backwards. 'But why did you lie?' he rasped. '*Why*?'

Tears welled up in her eyes again. 'At first I couldn't bring myself to believe you really loved me. And then I couldn't face hurting Sarah—taking away the one thing in her life which she had left to love. She has no one else, you see. No husband. No other children. No brothers or sisters. No one. Only me and Derek.

'I convinced myself you'd go away after you'd had some more sex. But then, when I was waiting for you to pick me up for dinner tonight and I became agitated about your being late, Sarah kept telling me not to worry—that Blind Freddie could see you cared about me, and Derek as well.

'I scoffed at her suggestions, but then you came, and you'd bought Derek those mobiles, and I saw that you might really love us. I just knew I couldn't go on seeing you and deceiving you. I didn't know what to do but send you away. But after you'd gone I just went crazy. I...I think I might have done something stupid, but Sarah made me pull myself together and insisted upon an explanation. She wouldn't take no for an answer for once, and in the end I told her everything.

'She...she was so brave about it, Luke. And so kind. She wasn't angry with me at all. She told me that she understood Patrick had not been a good husband, that he had been as difficult and as selfish a man as his own father. She also told me she loved Derek for himself, not his genes. She then insisted I find you and tell you the truth. It seems you told her this afternoon you were staying with your mother, who lived at Monterey, so I looked up her address in the phonebook and...and here I am.'

She sent him a despairing look. 'Can you ever forgive me, Luke?'

'Derek's my son,' was all he could say.

'Yes, my darling,' she murmured, and came to wind her arms around his waist, resting her head against his chest. '*Your* son. *Our* son.'

He wrapped his arms around her and closed his eyes. Never in all his life had he been this happy, or this sad. Eleven months wasted. All that love...wasted.

Don't look back, Luke, came the wise words of advice from deep inside. It's stupid and self-destructive. Looking forward is much, much better. If you think you've had a rotten time, think of her. God but she's had it hard. Time to make it easy for her. Time to prove your love.

He eased out of her embrace, smiling into her worried eyes while he started poking some stray strands of blonde hair behind her ears. 'I think that before I fully forgive you,' he began, 'I should extract a couple of promises.'

'Anything.'

'First thing tomorrow you will come with me while we look for a decent house to live in.'

Her face broke into the loveliest of smiles.

'Somewhere near here, so that my mother can visit her grandson. Something large enough to include a studio and a darkroom for myself and my photographic assistant-cum-model to work in. And somewhere that has a nice little self-contained flat attached for Sarah to live in. She is forthwith Derek's godmother and adopted grandmother.'

Rachel nodded, clearly all choked up with emotion and approval.

'Secondly, you will marry me as quickly as the proper paperwork can be done.'

She bit her bottom lip and nodded again.

'Meanwhile you are to do nothing to stop me conceiving a little brother or sister for Derek—starting with later tonight. Is that clear?'

'Perfectly clear,' she whispered, with an erotic little quiver.

Luke could not help himself. He had to kiss her at that point, although he rationed himself to only a couple of seconds. Any longer and he knew they'd both be in trouble.

'Do you realise I haven't told you yet that I love you?' he murmured against her oh, so willing mouth.

'Yes, you have, my darling,' she murmured back. 'You told me when you mowed my lawns and painted my carport. You told me when you bought our son those beautiful mobiles. You've been telling me all along, and I just refused to listen. But you can tell me again if you like,' she finished, and brushed her lips tantalisingly against his.

Damn, but she was a minx in that department!

'I love you, Rachel. I loved you from the first moment I saw you.'

'It must have been the same with me, Luke. I only hope your mother warms to the idea. I don't think she likes me very much.'

'She'll warm up to you soon enough, when she knows Derek's her grandson.'

'She already knows.'

'She *what*?'

'She guessed, Luke, after looking at Derek's photographs. She says they're the dead spit of you at the same age.'

'Ahh. Well, in that case, no problem. Mum's very large on family.'

'And very large on her favourite son.'

'What makes you say that?'

'Believe me, I know. But anyone who loves you that much is all right by me. Let's go and talk to her, Luke. She must be worried.'

'And then we'll drive down and talk to Sarah,' Luke suggested. 'She must be worried too. After which I'm going to wake up my son and talk to him. He doesn't like sleeping much anyway.'

'Luke St Clair—you're not going to be one of those fathers who spoil their children rotten, are you?'

'You'd better believe it, sweetheart. And I'm going to be one of those husbands who spoils his wife rotten too.'

'Oh, well, in that case, I have no objections. Spoil away!'

They opened the door of the bedroom, laughing together.

Grace heard the happy sounds from where she was sitting at the kitchen table and sighed a huge sigh of relief. Dashing the tears from her eyes, she slipped the photographs of her grandson into the family album, looking up just in time to see a smiling Luke bring Rachel into the room, his arm around her shoulders and his eyes full of love as he glanced over at her.

'Mum,' he began, 'say hello to your newest daughter-in-law.'

Grace's own smile came from the heart. 'How lovely,' she said, and rose to her feet, walking over to give Rachel a kiss on the cheek. 'Welcome to the family, my dear. I hope you'll both be very happy.'

Grace was moved by the look Rachel sent her son. So full of relief and love. She accepts me, it seemed to say. Everything is going to be all right.

And it was.

* * * * *

AFFAIRS TO REMEMBER: stories of love
you'll treasure forever.

HARLEQUIN PRESENTS®

Tully Cleaver was a good father, but was he husband material?

Find out in Daphne Clair's

#1866 *GROUNDS FOR MARRIAGE*

In our exciting new series

FROM HERE
TO PATERNITY

when men find their way to fatherhood by fair means, by foul or even by default!

Available in February wherever
Harlequin books are sold.

Take 4 bestselling love stories FREE

Plus get a FREE surprise gift!

Special Limited-time Offer

Mail to Harlequin Reader Service®

3010 Walden Avenue
P.O. Box 1867
Buffalo, N.Y. 14240-1867

YES! Please send me 4 free Harlequin Presents® novels and my free surprise gift. Then send me 6 brand-new novels every month, which I will receive months before they appear in bookstores. Bill me at the low price of $2.90 each plus 25¢ delivery and applicable sales tax, if any*. That's the complete price and a savings of over 10% off the cover prices—quite a bargain! I understand that accepting the books and gift places me under no obligation ever to buy any books. I can always return a shipment and cancel at any time. Even if I never buy another book from Harlequin, the 4 free books and the surprise gift are mine to keep forever.

106 BPA A3UL

Name	(PLEASE PRINT)	
Address	Apt. No.	
City	State	Zip

This offer is limited to one order per household and not valid to present Harlequin Presents® subscribers. *Terms and prices are subject to change without notice. Sales tax applicable in N.Y.

UPRES-696   ©1990 Harlequin Enterprises Limited